Frederick Marshall

Claire Brandon

A novel

Frederick Marshall

Claire Brandon
A novel

ISBN/EAN: 9783337051044

Printed in Europe, USA, Canada, Australia, Japan

Cover: Foto ©Andreas Hilbeck / pixelio.de

More available books at **www.hansebooks.com**

BY

FREDERICK MARSHALL

AUTHOR OF 'FRENCH HOME-LIFE,' ETC.

IN THREE VOLUMES

VOL. I.

WILLIAM BLACKWOOD AND SONS
EDINBURGH AND LONDON
MDCCCXC

CLAIRE BRANDON.

CHAPTER I.

On the afternoon of the 2d February 1862, Miss Harriet Brandon was sitting alone in the drawing-room of her cottage at Hurley. Her long, angular person was dressed in thick black silk. Her features were regular; her complexion was fresh; her expression was frank, generous, and rough. There was a distinct manifestation about her of the desire to be correct and dignified, and, mixed up with it, there was an irrepressible goodness and a detonating abruptness which contradicted the correct dignity. Her movements were somewhat hard and ungraceful, but yet she was unmistakably a lady. She had even, at certain moments, a marked distinction of bearing.

That afternoon she was out of temper, as happened to her frequently. Forty years of life had not calmed her tumultuous nature, and she had acquired amongst her neighbours the reputation of being as stormy as she was good, as explosive as she was free - hearted. She tried to read, but could not fix her attention, and pushed away the book. She poked the fire impatiently, and then sat and stared at it as if she expected peace of mind to issue from the smoke. While staring she heard wheels on the road outside. Half a minute later a carriage stopped at her door. She supposed a visitor was coming, so she hastily smoothed down her dress, tried, though with less success, to smooth down her face, and waited for the visitor to be announced. Vague sounds of talk reached her ears from the hall, but two minutes passed before a maid-servant opened the door and said—

"Please, ma'am, there is a foreign woman come in a fly from the station, and Morris's boy has brought her, and she has a baby with her, and I can't make out what she says, but she talks a great deal."

Miss Brandon looked at the maid and asked

her with as much indifference as she could command, " Is she a respectable person ? "

" Well, ma'am," answered the maid, " I shouldn't say she looks respectable, because she hasn't a bonnet. Only she seems decent, and I think she is tired, and she has got two boxes on the fly."

" For whom does she ask ? " inquired Miss Brandon.

" I can't understand her," was the reply.

Thereupon Miss Brandon got up and walked into the hall.

Standing there, with a child in her arms, was a middle-sized woman, wearing a dark shawl and dress, and a white muslin cap with white strings tied under her chin. Behind her was Morris's boy. As soon as the woman saw Miss Brandon she advanced eagerly towards her and asked in French, " Are you Miss Brandon ? "

It fortunately happened that Miss Brandon was able to speak French—not well, but sufficiently to understand and answer. So she replied, " Yes, I am Miss Brandon. What do you want ? "

The woman exclaimed with evident relief—

"Oh, mademoiselle, I have come a long way with the child. Poor child! And I am so glad to get here. The Colonel, he died at Lisbon. That is where I have come from. Only, Henry ought to have been with me; but he missed the steamer, and I have come alone. Henry, that is the Colonel's servant, mademoiselle. And I don't know how I got here. The Colonel, before he died, he told us both to come to his uncle and to mademoiselle, and to bring the child to you. And this is the child. Dear little child!" And she kissed it with much affection, and held it out for Miss Brandon to see.

Miss Brandon had listened to this speech with a stupefaction which had turned suddenly into a chill terror.

"The Colonel, he died at Lisbon!"

Could that mean that her brother, Colonel Charles Brandon, was dead?

She had not heard of him for a long time; she had no reason to suppose that he was ill; and though, for many years, she had only seen him at rare intervals, and had not kept up regular correspondence with him, she had a sincere attachment to him. So the sudden declaration made by the strange woman, coming, as it did, in the midst of one of her attacks of temper, made her heart beat and took her breath away, and it was almost with a sense of personal wrong being done to her that she cried out, "What colonel? Was it Colonel Charles Brandon? Was it my brother? And what child is this? And what does it all mean? Who are you?"

Miss Brandon seized a hall chair and sat down heavily, and her eyes filled with tears as she stared at the stranger.

"Yes," answered the woman, "it was the Colonel, my master, and this is his child. His name was Charles. That is true. It was a wound he had in a battle, that opened again, below his arm, because he had a fall at Cintra; and they brought him back very bad to Lisbon, to the hotel; and he could not write because he was ill and weak and his hand was hurt in the fall, so Henry wrote two letters for him and the Colonel signed them. And Henry took one of them—that one was for General Brandon—and there were papers put into it that were in a red box belonging to the Colonel; I saw that; and the Colonel

gave me the other one; and after he was dead
and buried, Henry took places for himself and
me in a steamer to come to England, as the
Colonel told us to do, to bring the letters and
the child. After Henry had put me and the
child and the luggage on board, he returned
on shore again to fetch something he had forgotten. I went to bed with the child, and
then I was awoke by the steamer moving and
making a noise, and I was very ill. A woman
came and helped me with the child. Two
days afterwards I got better, and I was able
to go on deck, and I looked for Henry. But
I could not see him. And I found some one
to speak for me, and I inquired, and was told
that Henry had not come on board again, and
that the steamer could not wait, and had
started without him. So I cried, and I cried
for a long time, for I was all alone there with
the child. There were some people who were
very kind to me, and spoke to me, and tried to
comfort me, and said that Henry would come
by the next steamer. And I told them the
Colonel was dead, and that I was taking the
child to the family. So when we reached the
port—Southampton it was—the kind people
changed my money for me—it was my own

money, mademoiselle, for Henry had got the Colonel's money—and put me into the train, and gave me a piece of paper with the name and address of mademoiselle which were on the letter, and told the guard about me, and he made me get out at the station, and then the station-master looked at the paper and got the boxes for me, and spoke to a boy that was there — this boy — and he put me into a carriage, and the boy brought me here. This is the child." And she began to cry.

The woman had poured out this long speech with extreme rapidity and growing agitation. It was clear that she had gone through strong emotions, and was so much upset that her head was not quite clear. But Miss Brandon was far too excited herself to think of any one else. She had listened to the story with intense attention, but yet with an almost irresistible longing to interrupt and to ask questions. So, the moment the woman stopped, Miss Brandon jumped off her chair, rushed close up to her, and staring her in the face as if she were an enemy, gasped out a string of disconnected interrogatories, which were rendered almost incomprehensible by the insufficiency of her French.

" Why is my brother dead ?   And how do I know that he is dead ?   Who are you that I should believe you ?   And when did he die ? Oh, when did he die ?   Who was with him at his last moments ?   When will the other servant arrive ?   But you said you had a letter for me from my brother.   Where is that letter ?   Are you an impostor ?"

The woman listened, and it was plain that she tried to understand ; but the word "letter" was the only one that seemed to strike her, for, without answering one word to the dishevelled questions flung at her, she clutched the child with her left arm, put her right hand into her pocket and drew out, after some fumbling, a little parcel tied in a piece of newspaper.

Miss Brandon instantly snatched it from her, and, with trembling hands, tore off the paper. Inside she found a letter addressed to

Miss Brandon,

    Hurley,

        near Lorston,

            Hants.

In excitement which almost prevented her from seeing clear, she broke open the envelope, pulled out the letter, and read the following words :—

"LISBON, BRAGANZA HOTEL,
17th *January* 1862.

" MY DEAR SISTER,—My wound has opened again, from a fall ; my lungs have become congested, and I fear I shall not recover.

" As I am unable to write myself, I dictate this to Henry Blaine, my old servant, in whom I have entire confidence.

" I have to confess to you that I was married, three years ago, to a French lady. I have not acknowledged it, because my uncle's feelings against foreigners and Roman Catholics are so strong.

" At the end of twelve months of happiness my wife died, in giving birth to a child.

" My wife had no relations. There was no one to whom I could confide the child. Nor, indeed, did I wish to part from it. So I wandered about the Continent, writing from time to time to my uncle to say that I was coming home soon. The truth was that I was in ex-

treme sadness and in failing health. I came
here for the winter, with my child.

"All I can do now is to bequeath the
child to your care. Be good to her, for my
sake.

"She is called Claire—her mother's name.
She must be brought up as a Roman Cath-
olic, because I pledged myself to that when
I married.

"This will be given to you by Berthe, the
nurse, who is a kind woman.

"I send another letter, with all the papers
and particulars of my marriage, by Henry, to
my uncle. I ask my uncle to forgive me and
to adopt my child.

"Farewell, my dear sister.

"May God bless you and my poor child.—
Your most affectionate brother,

"CHARLES BRANDON."

When Miss Brandon got to the end of the
letter, she dropped her hands and looked silently at the ground. She was so dazed that
she was incapable of thinking. But, after a
moment, her natural excitability burst out
again, and she turned, almost angrily, to the

nurse, exclaiming, "You have not shown me the child. Show her to me."

The woman raised her towards Miss Brandon. The child looked, hesitated, and then stretched out her little hand and took hold of Miss Brandon's chin.

This was too much for the poor lady's nerves. She burst violently into tears (she did everything with vehemence, even crying), seized the child, covered it with kisses, and dashed off with it suddenly to the drawing-room, calling to the nurse to follow her. Fortunately the child did not complain, and remained quiet. Miss Brandon caressed her awkwardly, muttered some inaudible words which were meant to be affectionate, and then, twisting sharply round, said, half hysterically, "Now sit down there and tell me all about it. I don't understand at all. When did he marry? Who was his wife? Why did he tell me nothing? How long was he ill? What did he say your name is?"

The answer came in language almost as excited as that in which the questions were put: "I have never seen the mother. I only entered the Colonel's service after her death.

I know nothing about her. Nobody told me anything. Henry is coming and will explain, for he knows."

" But I can't wait," replied Miss Brandon, almost shouting in her emotion. " I must know at once. It is all so sudden and so strange. Now tell me all you do know."

" Well, mademoiselle, I took the child a year ago last month, when she was weaned. The Colonel was at Versailles then. He sent away the wet nurse before I came, so I had no talk with her. We travelled to several places, and went to Lisbon for the winter, because the Colonel had a cough. He loved the child very much, and used to hold it on his knee and whisper to it in English. He was always very sad, and Henry told me he had never got over madame's death, and that he never would. But Henry could speak only a few words of French, and I don't think he liked to talk to me about it. Perhaps the Colonel told him not to do so. And I asked no questions, and I never heard anything at all, except that madame had died in France when the baby was born."

" This is all very strange," said Miss Brandon, disappointed and vexed at the absence of immediate information. Very strange. And so horribly sudden. I must consult my uncle. How angry he will be ! I am quite afraid to let him know. But I must. I suppose you had better put the child to bed. I will tell the housemaid to sit with it while you have something to eat. Of course you will stop here for the present."

Miss Brandon rang, and ordered that the flyman should be paid, the luggage brought in, and a room got ready for the nurse and child, whom she sent up-stairs. When that was arranged she sat down, with much apprehension, and wrote to General Brandon, who lived a mile off, at Hurley Park, begging him to come over to her as soon as possible. Then she read her brother's letter again, cried over it, and muttered—"Poor Charles ! How could he do so ! And how sad for him to die all alone, so far away ! And this poor little child ! How sad ! how sad ! And I shall have to bring her up ; I, who know nothing about children. I must ask Uncle William for advice. How violent he will be ! And what a shock and disappointment to him ! But I must tell him, whatever be the consequences."

She got up and walked about the room, and sat down again, and read the letter a third time, and took up a paper-cutter and tapped her fingers with it, and then, instinctively, pushed by a force she could not resist, she went up-stairs after the child, and helped to undress it, and kissed it a good deal.

In taking off the child's clothes she saw round its neck, on a thin chain, a little gold medal, such as most Catholic children wear. It bore on one side a figure of the Virgin, and on the other the letters C. B. and the date 1st April 1860.

"Her initials, and the day of her birth," said the nurse. "I believe her father put it on her when she was born."

At six o'clock General Brandon drove up. He was a very old man, with a hard but intelligent face, expressive of much energy and will; he was straight and well preserved, and looked, in spite of his years, as if he might last a long time.

"What is it, Harriet?" he asked, testily. "Why do you send for me in this way? And with no explanations. You know I hate coming out on winter evenings."

" My dear uncle, I should not have disturbed
you—you may be sure of that—if something
particular had not happened. I have received
bad news—very bad news—which will grieve
you as much as it does me. It is about
. . . Charlie——" and then she broke down
and stopped to sob.

"What is the matter with Charlie?" exclaimed the General? But after a few seconds
he understood. "Charlie dead! Good God!
Where? When? Was it that wound? But
is that it? Is he really dead? Or is it something else? And how do you know it?"

"Yes, that is it; he is dead," moaned Miss
Brandon. "He has died at Lisbon. The wound
reopened. But he was ill before. And, my
dear uncle, that is not all. There is something
else besides. It seems that without saying anything to any of us . . . he had got married."

"Got married!" shouted the old General,
springing to his feet. "Got married! And
without telling *me?* Got married without
telling *me?* Why, he was my heir. His
duty was to tell me, and everybody else too.
What does it mean, Harriet? Why didn't he
tell me?"

" My dear uncle, there is a letter for you on the road, telling you all about it. All the details are in it, but it has not arrived yet. I know it by another letter which poor Charlie sent to me, and which got here this afternoon. It came faster than yours. A person brought it. And . . . and there is some more to tell you, only don't be angry. Charlie, poor Charlie, had a child, and he has sent the child to me, and it is up-stairs."

" Good God ! " groaned the General. " That Charlie should have deceived me in this way ! That he should have hidden all this from me, knowing that he was my heir ! And he wrote to me from time to time to say he was coming home, for he knew I wanted him, and he told me he had still some places to see before he settled down at Hurley. That was his excuse. I see it now. Very wrong ! very wrong ! It is horrible that Charlie should have told me lies."

" But, my dear uncle, perhaps he did it all for a good motive; perhaps he thought it might pain you."

" Pain me ? Why should it have pained me if it was a proper marriage ? Naturally, he

ought to have married, and to have children;
for he knew, as well as you do, that the property was to go to him and his heirs, and not
to George, or to the other branch of the family.
But . . . Harriet . . . I am afraid I am beginning to understand. It was not a proper
marriage! Is that the reason? Tell me."

"Oh yes, it was a proper marriage; quite a
proper marriage; at least . . . I don't know . . .
but I think so. The person who has arrived
is ignorant of the details, but the letter I have
received says his wife was . . . a French lady."

"French? French?" roared the General.
"He married a Frenchwoman? Harriet, I
understand now why he did not tell me."

"Well, it is not a crime to be French.
There must be French people, just as there are
other people. Only, as she was French, she
was . . . a Roman Catholic."

"She was a Papist too!" yelled the General,
his voice growing more violent at each ejacu-
lation. "Well, Harriet, if that was the case,
Charles was right not to tell me. I wouldn't
have received her, nor him either."

"Oh, my dear uncle, don't say that; pray
don't. Poor Charlie is dead."

"Dead!—the best thing that could have happened to him. Only, now the property must go to George. And, pray, where is his French wife?"

"She is dead too."

"Oh, if she is dead, the matter is not so bad after all," growled the General, still wild with passion, but perceptibly relieved by the last detail.

"But the child is here, Uncle William; it has just gone to sleep. It is a dear little child. And she will love you, and you will love her, instead of Charlie."

"Love a French Papist's child! I! Don't talk nonsense, Harriet. I hate the French, and I hate Papists. You know I do. And I shall not change."

"But do remember that it is Charlie's child. Poor little thing! Well, the other letter, the one that Charlie has written to you, will be here in a few days, and then we shall learn all about it. Here is the letter Charlie wrote to me when he was dying. It is about the child. Won't you read it?"

So the General read it, and muttered over it. But he was quieter, and after a little reflection, said—" Great loss, Harriet ; great loss. I don't at all like the property going to George. You know I don't like George. I never did. Nobody does. And this death of Charlie makes me very sad. Of course he ought to have outlived me, and to have inherited the estate. I was very fond of Charlie. And now he is dead. I suspect, too, that I see his real motive for secrecy. He thought I should die soon—I am eighty-one—and that, when once I was out of the way, his marriage would not matter."

As he spoke, the old man's lips trembled, a sign of emotion he had perhaps never displayed in his whole previous life.

Profiting by this symptom of feeling, Miss Brandon put her arm on her uncle's shoulder and asked, with as much softness as her nature could assume, if he would go up and see the child. He did not refuse.

They found the little thing asleep. They looked at it in silence. Miss Brandon's eyes filled once more with tears ; she longed to wake the child and cover it with kisses. The General was very grave. But when, on turning round to leave the room,

he caught sight of the nurse dozing in a cor-
ner, he growled between his teeth—"Horrid
Frenchwoman!"

They went down - stairs together. In the
hall the General said, with manifest sadness,
"I will come back in the morning. Poor
Charlie! Good night, Harriet."

Miss Brandon went again to the side of the
child's bed, and sat there for two hours in a
half - dazed state, feeling vaguely that something new had come into her life.

The next day the General walked down
early to the cottage. He looked very tired,
and his manner showed distress and anxiety.
His first words were—"I have been thinking
unceasingly about all this, Harriet. I have
scarcely slept at all. I am very much
worried. All my plans are upset. You
know that when I made my will, I left
Hurley and everything else to Charles, or,
failing him, to his heir-at-law; and, foolishly,
I did not specify a male heir, for I took it
for granted he would have a boy. I shall
have to make another will now, and to leave
Hurley to your brother George. He is now
the male heir. I don't like him, and I never

meant him to have the estate, but really I can't give it to this child, a girl, and to be brought up a Papist too. No, Harriet, I can't do that. I will make a good provision for the child, to be added to what comes to her from her father, but she cannot have Hurley. That is impossible, and I must alter it. But it is most disagreeable to me to have to leave the place to George. I must go in to Lorston and talk about it to Cumber, and give him instructions to prepare another will for me to sign. I am afraid I must do that, Harriet. Not that I like it. Oh no ; quite the contrary. I don't like it at all. And then I am so sorry about Charles. I really am. But why did he keep his marriage secret from me ? It was so wrong of him ; and it looks so false. And a Frenchwoman and a Papist too."

" My dear uncle, he kept it secret precisely because she was French and a Catholic. He did not dare to tell you. I see, with great relief, that, because they are both dead, you are disposed to forgive dear Charlie. But suppose they were both alive, uncle ? What then ? Would you have forgiven Charlie in that case ? "

"No, certainly not," was the unhesitating reply.

"Shall I bring Claire to you?" asked Miss Brandon, thinking it wise to change the subject.

"Claire? Who is Claire? Oh, the child! You have got very quickly to calling it Claire. A French name!"

"Yes, but it is her name; and it is a short and convenient name. And Clare, without an *i*, is English too; so, as the pronunciation is the same, no one will know it is a French name."

"Yes—I shall," said the General. "I shall never forget it."

Miss Brandon fetched the child, who, though not pretty, looked fresh and pleasant. She was certainly a winning child, and had nice ways.

The General looked keenly at her for some moments, and murmured—"And this is all that is left of Charlie! Of that brave boy Charlie! This poor little thing, that has been sent from one country to another to find a home, and from one woman to another to find a mother!"

" She shall find both here ! " exclaimed Miss Brandon impetuously, kissing the child with such eagerness that she made it cry for the first time.

The nurse had to be sent for to quiet her. She looked all the better for a good sleep and clean clothes, and her appearance, though shockingly foreign in the General's eyes, was so respectable that he was constrained to observe—" Seems a decent woman, Harriet, all the same. Better keep her till you get a good English nurse. Now I'll go to Lorston and see what is to be done. I'll come back here to lunch and tell you what Cumber says."

Mr Cumber was a solicitor of much experience, and as a result of that experience, would never give advice to his clients, even when it was asked for, as to what they should do with their money. So when the General consulted him about the change in his will, the only answer he could get was—" Tell me what you wish, General, and I will prepare a draft for your approval. It is your business to decide how your property is to be left; it is mine to put your intentions into form."

This was not at all what the General
wanted, for at the bottom of his heart he
hoped Mr Cumber would make objections to
the plan of leaving the estate to his nephew
George Brandon. But he would not own to
Mr Cumber that he felt so; and as no opening
offered itself for discussing any other arrangement, he tried to persuade himself that he
was satisfied, talked about the necessity of a
male heir for an estate that had been five
hundred years in the family, though it had
never been entailed, and finally gave verbal
instructions to Mr Cumber to draw up a new
will, leaving Hurley Park, with the woods
and farms, to George Brandon, £40,000 in
consols and railway debentures to the child
Claire as daughter and heir of Charles Brandon,
confirming a legacy of £20,000, mentioned in
the first will, in favour of Harriet Brandon,
and leaving the rest of the personalty for
equal division between George and Harriet
Brandon.

Then the General drove back to his niece,
feeling extremely discontented, and in that
state of peevishness into which so many old
people fall if their arrangements are disturbed,

and if they are obliged by circumstances to do
what is disagreeable to them.

He stated what he had done, grumbled that
he had had to do it, and said he was utterly
disgusted to be obliged to leave the estate to
George. And then he went into a rambling
complaint against Charles Brandon, as the
cause of all these worries ; said he had been
deceived by him, and worked himself by
degrees into a passion, in which he used a
good deal of strong language.

Harriet Brandon took all this with unusual
calmness, defended her brother in moderate
words, and tried to quiet the General by once
more proposing that he should go with her to
the child. This time, however, the stratagem
did not succeed. The old gentleman not only
refused to see the baby then, but declared, with
a good deal of ferocity, that he would never
see it any more, that the sight of it was odious
to him, and that the sooner it was sent away
the better he would be pleased.

Instead of meeting this ill-temper by similar
violence of her own, as she would have done
twenty-four hours before, Miss Brandon attempted very earnestly to soothe her uncle,

answered his outbursts with gentleness, and succeeded at last in getting him in to luncheon in a comparatively appeased state. But the pacification was only superficial; the General was altogether upset, ate very little, complained of headache, said he wanted to be alone, and went away in recommencing excitement.

As soon as he was gone, Miss Brandon returned to the child, took it on her knee, and began to talk to it. For the first time she felt tenderness growing up within her.

She had been left an orphan when she was very young, and had been brought up by a distant relative of disagreeable character; at twenty-one she had come into the possession of £1200 a-year, had settled with a companion in the cottage at Hurley, had not found a husband, and, as the years passed on, had grown irritable, and even harsh in manner. And yet at the bottom of her heart there was infinite goodness hidden away, awaiting satisfying employment, and flinging itself out meanwhile in capricious kindness to the poor people round. There was more than goodness in her; there was a need of love which would have frightened her if she had been able to analyse her feelings, and to measure and understand the true extent of her own capacity for affection. She had been led by destiny to imagine that she was cold; no circumstance in her dry, solitary life had ever struck her heart-strings, had ever made her vibrate, had ever proved to her that, like many other untried women, she possessed a temperament that on occasion could bring forth great fruit, a power of sympathy and devotion, and even of enthusiasm and passion, as real and as potential, in their dormant unconsciousness, as if fate had called upon them, through long years, to prove in action their efficacy and their force. The world of lonely women is full to overflowing of latent unsuspected capabilities of love. More fortunate than many others, Harriet Brandon had found her opportunity at last. But she did not know it yet.

In ignorance of her own ability of attachment, believing from pure inexperience that she had no soul to pour out in fondness, she took the baby and whispered nonsense to it, thinking that was the right way to behave to it. And even her nonsense confirmed her, at

first, in the conviction that she had no tenderness to offer, for it seemed to her most awk-
ward, chilly nonsense, quite unworthy to be
used to such a fresh, bright baby. She fancied,
in her utter unskilfulness, that the child would
perceive how incapable she was, which, considering that it was twenty-two months old,
was scarcely a reasonable supposition. Instead, however, of seeming discontented, it
stared at her, and laughed, as if it compre-
hended and approved; it threw its arms into
the air with evident joyousness, and Miss
Brandon began to feel less humiliated, and
even somewhat encouraged, and kissed and
talked and endeavoured to tell stories, and
found that the occupation, though quite new
to her, was singularly pleasant.

And as she kissed and babbled, the thought
came suddenly before her that this baby, which
had fallen to her from the skies the day before,
was absolutely her own; that she had got it
all to herself, that she could do what she liked
with it, that its destiny depended in great
part upon her will. This abrupt perception
of the nature and the responsibilities of maternity gave at first a shock of fear to Miss Bran-

don, who conscientiously believed herself to be
totally unfit for the duties thrust upon her,
and who had not yet discovered that a duty
which is based on love can never frighten.
The duty was there before her, in all its
suddenly alarming vastness; the love that
was to lighten and to brighten it, and to
make of it a joy of the intensest reality and
purity, had not yet formed in her sufficiently
to cheer her. She saw the duty by itself,
and for an instant shrank from it in awe.
But yearning was already arising within her,
insensibly though rapidly, and she found to
her astonishment, as the moments passed, that
she fondled more and feared less, and, soon,
that all fear had disappeared. She told herself that she had a charge. The notion came
to her tumultuously, and was seized by her
with her usual impetuosity. Thoughts dashed
about in her, and shook her, and made her
tremble, but yet, notwithstanding their effer-
vescence, they were altogether clear; there
was no mist about them; they stood out
sharply before her, and she found delight in
them. She did not realise, for the moment,
the immensity of the change that had been

wrought in her, but she knew that she had
suddenly a mission, and she rejoiced. An
unaccustomed sentiment of peace began to
pervade her heart; a consciousness that she
was no longer alone in life developed itself in
the air around her; she seemed to breathe it,
and infinitely sweet it was to her. Love had
not come into her in an instantaneous bursting
flood, as it rushes into the mother when she
hears the first feeble cry of her new-born
child; in her case it had needed a few hours
for its formation. The hours had passed, and
the love had come, and Harriet Brandon held
out the child at arm's length, and gazed at it
with a swelling in her heart; and suddenly
a great resistless wave of tenderness passed
over her—she ceased to chatter nonsense, and
gravely said, " Claire, I love you."

Claire laughed, but did not understand.

And then Miss Brandon, more gravely still,
with tears rolling unnoticed down her cheeks,
said once more, in the child's mother's tongue,
as if she were a priestess performing a religious
rite, and were solemnly taking possession of the
child in its mother's place, " Claire, je t'aime."

But Claire went on laughing, and did not

understand that either. She only stretched
out her little hands and waved them about.

Miss Brandon murmured to herself, "She
can never call me mother. That would be
too great a joy; a greater joy than I deserve.
But, Charlie, you have left her to my care,
and I will do my duty to her—as if I were
her mother."

And, sobbing, she carried the baby to its
bed, and laid it down, and knelt beside it,
and prayed with all her might.

She rose up strangely comforted, feeling,
confusedly, for the first time in her existence,
that gentleness was now a need of her career,
and was on the point of taking the baby into
her arms once more, and of going on whisper-
ing to it of the new love that possessed her,
when rapid steps came up the staircase, the
door was opened hastily, and the maid sprang
in, exclaiming, "Oh, ma'am, such bad news!
The General has been taken in a fit, and they
think he is dying. A man has run down from
the House to tell you."

CHAPTER II.

BEFORE Miss Brandon could reach the House, the General was dead. The violent emotions he had gone through had been too much for him, and had brought on apoplexy.

The shock to Miss Brandon was very severe. She was warmly attached to her uncle, with whom she had lived, for many years, in almost daily contact; and, naturally, the effect which had been produced on her excitable temperament by the news of her brother's death and by the arrival of the child, had rendered her more than ordinarily nervous, and quite unfit to bear a new blow. She sobbed most violently, and was utterly upset. But yet her will was strong enough to make her perceive that she ought to telegraph to her brother George, announcing the double loss of his uncle and his brother, and asking him to come at once to

Hurley. And then she went back home, and sat at the child's side, and cried.

The next afternoon Mr George Brandon appeared. He was ten years younger than his sister. He was a barrister, and lived in London. He was intelligent, well-mannered, and good-looking, and yet he was generally disliked. No one, however, could have explained why. There was no apparent reason for the antipathy he provoked. He had never done anything wrong to anybody. It was true that there were lurking signs of sourness and falseness about his mouth ; that his chin had a distinctly aggressive expression, resulting from the hardness and the sharpness of its lines ; and that his eyes had often an unquiet look, as if he were conscious of a crime and expected to be suddenly arrested : but these indications were not marked enough or evident enough to attract attention, or to show that he had a character which justified people in shrinking from him. As he sought no intimacies and possessed no friends, nobody was sufficiently interested in him to ask the motive of the instinctive dislike that was felt towards him. His sister, who mistrusted him profoundly, was probably the only person who could give an explanation of her aversion. She was perfectly clear and very outspoken on the subject; she concealed from no one that, in her opinion, her brother George had no heart at all, that he thought of nothing but himself, and that he passed his time in unceasing preoccupation as to the means he could employ to turn things to his own advantage. Her own nature was so open, so generous, so impulsive, that the calculating coldness of her brother disgusted her, and made her feel ashamed that any one of the name of Brandon should be constituted in such a fashion. His presence irritated her and always stimulated her quarrelsomeness. The result was that his visits to her had been rare.

When he came in they kissed each other coldly.

Mr George Brandon observed, "All this is very sad, Harriet; very sad."

And Miss Brandon replied, "Yes, George, very sad; extremely sad."

And then they seemed to have no more to say.

After a while it occurred to Miss Brandon

that it would be right to communicate to her
brother the details of the events which had
just happened. So she told him the whole
story. He listened with close attention, and,
when she had finished, remained silent for a
time.

At last he remarked, in a tone of voice
which seemed to her peculiarly acrimonious,
"Then, as my uncle did not live to execute
the new will, I am excluded from the property
he meant me to have, and this child, as
Charles's heir-at-law, comes into Hurley under
the provisions of the old will."

"Of course," replied Miss Brandon, who,
until that moment, had not given a thought
to this aspect of the situation, but who felt
suddenly quite comforted by the notion that
George was bitterly disappointed.

And then there was another silence, during
which Miss Brandon hesitated whether she
should ask him to see the child. It seemed
to her that, on the whole, it was right to do
so, and therefore she proposed to him to go
up-stairs with her.

He, however, declined the offer, saying,
"Thank you, Harriet; I think not. You

really can scarcely expect me to have much
liking for a child who has dropped from God
knows where between me and seven thousand
a-year."

This answer, which was perhaps not altogether inexcusable under the circumstances,
appeared to Miss Brandon to be so abominably
and so unpardonably wicked, that a furious
answer rushed instantly to her lips. But
something checked her, something new within
her—she did not know what. She made,
instinctively, an effort to control herself, swal-
lowed twice convulsively, and said nothing.

As soon as the funeral was over, Mr George
Brandon returned to London, after an icy
parting with his sister.

Mr Cumber had been appointed by the will
executor and trustee, and, in those qualities,
proceeded to enter into possession of the estate
for the child.

And then, when the business was done,
Miss Brandon threw her whole self into the
child. She forgot the sadness of the two
recent deaths, she forgot her duties in the
village, she forgot entirely to get angry several
times a-day. She lived for nothing else than

to look at Claire, and play with her, and
chatter to her.   But, as the nurse was a necessary part of Claire, she talked to her as well,
and got technical instruction from her about
the handling of a baby, and listened to her
stories about the Colonel, and began to like her.

In one of their conversations the nurse observed, "Don't you think, mademoiselle, it is
time that Henry arrived ?   It seems to me he
ought to be here now."

" Of course he ought," replied Miss Brandon.
" You came nearly a fortnight ago.   Of course
he ought to be here.   I will ask Mr Cumber
when the boat is due."

She went that afternoon to Lorston for the
purpose, and was told by Mr Cumber that he
too was rather surprised at the delay, and that
he thought it would be as well to communicate
with the agents at Southampton in order to
ascertain the day on which the steamer was
expected.   A letter was sent by him at once.

The answer came by return of post, stating
that not only the vessel following the Britannia
(which had brought the nurse and child), but
another also had come in, and that Henry
Blaine was not on board either of them.   The

letter added that Blaine's luggage had remained
unclaimed since it had been landed from the
Britannia, and that Mr Cumber (who was
known to the agents) had better have it taken
away to avoid warehouse expenses.

This news perplexed Mr Cumber. He felt
instinctively, as a lawyer, that it would be
just as well—if only as a matter of form—to
have the papers Blaine was bringing, and
though delay was of no real importance, still
it was useless and vexing. And Blaine, too,
was to tell the whole story of the marriage,
and to give Miss Brandon the details she was
waiting for with such eagerness. Until he
came she would have to remain in ignorance.
His non - arrival seemed inexplicable, and,
whatever was the cause of it, was certainly
particularly annoying.

There was, at that time, no cable to Lisbon,
otherwise Mr Cumber would have asked the
people at Southampton to inquire by it what
had become of Henry Blaine. The mails went
by sea, and as the boats were only weekly and
took five days for the passage, two or three
weeks might elapse before an answer could be
got by post. Still, though it seemed unneces-

sary to write—because it was taken for granted that Blaine was on the way somewhere—the agents were requested to obtain news from Lisbon.

Meanwhile the luggage was sent for. There were several packages : two of them bore the name of Henry Blaine ; the rest had belonged to Colonel Brandon.

In the presence of Miss Harriet Brandon, at Mr Cumber's office, all the trunks were broken open. It was a painful proceeding, and Miss Brandon suffered keenly from it ; but her surmise that her brother's letter to the General might be in Blaine's boxes, and her confident expectation that, in any event, she would find information about the marriage amongst her brother's papers, gave her courage to go through with the task. The red despatch-box of which the nurse had spoken was soon found, but, to the vexation of Miss Brandon, it contained nothing of the faintest interest. There were no letters, no documents, no indications of any kind. The few memoranda that were in it were notes about Portugal in the Colonel's writing, and some calculations of the time and expense necessary for a journey to Oporto and

the Minho.   In the portmanteaus there were
clothes and personal objects and a few books,
but nothing that had the slightest relation to
family affairs.   It was therefore with much
increased interest, and even agitation, that
Miss Brandon turned to the two boxes belonging to the servant, in the eager hope that the
letter would be there.   But again she was
disappointed; there was nothing in Blaine's
luggage that could throw the slightest light
upon the situation.   There was a letter from
his mother, with news of the coming marriage
of his sister, and that was all.

Miss Brandon went back to Hurley extremely mortified and saddened, and with a
strong disposition to lose her temper on the
first opportunity that might offer.   Mr Cumber
had not attempted to console her; he had
simply observed, "Well, now, we must wait
till Blaine arrives."

But, as waiting is generally an irritating
process, as it had always been particularly so
to Miss Brandon, and as the circumstances
were of a nature to intensify its effects, it
put her into such a state of nervousness and
impatience that even the child ceased to ex-

ercise a quieting influence over her. She went in almost every day to Lorston, to see Mr Cumber, and persecuted him with questions. She exaggerated or mistook the meanings of the prudent, guarded answers he made to her, and worked herself into a state of irrepressible agitation. She began to suspect there was some deceit about the whole story from Lisbon. She attacked the nurse and told her she was an impostor and a liar; and then she grew suddenly ashamed and sorry, and begged the woman to take no notice of her words, because she did not mean what she said. Sometimes she doubted whether her brother was dead, whether the letter she had received was really from him, whether he had ever been married, and whether the child was his at all. At other moments she became passionately loving with Claire, called her by all the names that tenderness could invent, and cried for hours over her. Then she addressed a hundred questions to the nurse, and obtained no reply. This state of things went on until more than a month had passed since the arrival of the child; but still there was no sign of Henry Blaine.

At last, one afternoon, Mr Cumber appeared at the cottage. He looked serious, and Miss Brandon felt instinctively that something had happened.

He brought her two letters he had received that day. One was from the steamboat agents at Southampton, enclosing a copy of the answer from their house at Lisbon. It stated simply that nothing had been heard of Blaine since the departure of the Britannia. The other, from Mr George Brandon, was as follows :—

" LONDON, 6*th* March 1862.

"MY DEAR CUMBER,—I suppose my brother's servant has arrived with the papers concerning his marriage.

" As I have received no communication from you on the subject, I shall be much obliged if you will have the kindness to inform me about it.—Sincerely yours,

" GEORGE BRANDON."

After reading the two letters, Miss Brandon exclaimed, with an emotion which grew more and more violent as she went on speaking, and reached at last a paroxysm of excitement :

"What can it all mean? What can have become of Blaine? Certainly there must be something wrong. Can Blaine have got up the whole story for some purpose of his own? How do we know that Charles really signed that letter to me? Oh, pray advise me! What shall I do? Of course I shall keep the dear little child; but is it Charlie's child at all? Oh, do tell me what to do! And George? It is manifest that he will make difficulties if he can. I felt that the first time I saw him after my uncle's death. But—Mr Cumber—if George makes difficulties, that will change everything? In that case, I will defend the child, no matter what happens. I cannot bear George, and if he turns against the little darling, I will fight him, although he is my brother. Besides, I have no doubts at all. I did not mean it when I said I had. I know it is Charlie's child, and I know he was married, and feel it is all true, as if I had been a witness. Who can dispute it? Nobody would, except George. He is so odiously selfish, George. If he means to be hostile to the baby, he will provoke me to the bitterest resistance. I will stand before her as if she

were my own—and she is my own. I have
sworn that to poor Charlie. Now tell me, Mr
Cumber, what shall we do?"

"Well, my dear lady, I have of course given
a good deal of thought to the matter. It is,
as you say, very strange, and I do not pretend
to understand it. All that we can do for the
moment is to try to discover, if possible, what
has become of Blaine. For that purpose, I
propose to you to send out a person to Lisbon.
If that is not done, and if Blaine's arrival
continues to be delayed, we may remain
indefinitely in our present condition of uncertainty. I have a very intelligent clerk,
who can speak a little French, and if you
authorise the expense, I think he had better
go by the next boat, and try to get to the
bottom of the matter. His name is Gray. I
know no one else so fit to be intrusted with
such a mission."

The proposal calmed Miss Brandon a little,
for it opened the door to action, and in that
way gave a sort of satisfaction to the energy
of her character. She answered, "Certainly;
I quite agree with you. Of course we cannot
go on in this way; it is altogether intolerable.

Pray send Mr Gray at once. I shall be so much obliged to you. And tell him, above all, not to lose an instant in letting us know. My anxiety is becoming so intense, that at moments I can scarcely bear it. And what answer will you send to George? Oh, how wicked he is!"

" I can only say the truth—that Blaine has not arrived, that we are expecting him every day, and that I will let Mr George know as soon as he is here."

Then Mr Cumber went away, and Miss Brandon walked up and down the room, and thought. "I know what George is about," she said to herself. " He is seeking for means to attack Charlie's child—my child. To attack my child! And he calls himself my brother! And all for money. How hideous! Well, poor Charlie! you would not have expected that. Of course it is impossible to understand the absence of the servant; and if George had behaved properly, I might have had doubts myself. But his letter to Cumber has made all my doubts disappear. If he had any heart he would have no suspicions, but would join with me in protecting the child, instead of

working against the little darling for his
own odious purposes. Little darling! I will
take care of you. It steadies me and quiets
me to think that the duty of defending you
has fallen to me. And defend you I will, to
the utmost limit of energy and effort. It is
my duty. Sweet little innocent! How cruel
that you should be treated in this way by my
own brother!"

Miss Brandon forgot, in her indignation,
that, so far, her brother George had simply
asked Mr Cumber, in the most natural manner,
for information, and had manifested no intentions whatever. But her way of reasoning
did not always take facts for a basis; it
was her habit to be illogical and to jump to
extremes, and in this case her pre-existing
dislike of her brother disposed her to view
his proceedings in the worst light. She sus-
pected that, if he could, he would dispute
the rights of the child, and the suspicion
rendered her wild. It had appeared to her
quite natural to feel, at certain moments, misgivings and hesitations herself; but the instant
she fancied that any one else shared them,
she got into a rage, and declared it was dis-

graceful to have any doubts at all. And it was especially disgraceful in her eyes that her own brother—who certainly had the strongest possible motives for desiring to be able to doubt —should permit himself to ask for news.

In feverish agitation she had to wait for intelligence from Lisbon. She scarcely ever left the child. Her love for it became almost a frenzy. She grew frightened if it was out of her sight for a few minutes, and imagined sometimes that attempts would be made to steal it. She had it in her room at night, and was perpetually starting in her sleep, and getting out of bed to put her arms round it, in order to protect it. The nurse complained, and said this woke the child; but she had found already that it was useless to resist Miss Brandon, and recognised that she must either bear it all, or go. So, not wishing to go, she bore it. Besides, Miss Brandon treated her, as a rule, most kindly, and talked to her continually; they wondered together where Blaine could be, and what had become of the letter, and, in a sort of way, they became friends under the pressure of their common anxiety.

At last, after wearying suspense, a letter came from Mr Gray. It was as follows :—

"LISBON, 24th March 1862.

"SIR,—I arrived here on the 18th instant, and, according to your instructions, went at once to the Braganza Hotel, and to the British Legation and Consulate.

"As soon as I had stated the object of my journey, I received offers of assistance from every one. The Consul was kind enough to place a clerk at my disposal, to go about with me, and interpret for me.

"At the hotel I learnt that Colonel Brandon died there on 18th January, and that he was buried on the 20th. I have seen the two doctors who attended him, and was told by them that the immediate cause of death was pneumonia, brought on by the reopening of the wound in the side, following on a previous condition of disease of the lungs. I have obtained a duly authenticated certificate of the death.

"The Colonel appears to have shown very remarkable affection to the child during the time he was in Lisbon. His tenderness was

so unceasing, that it was noticed by all the
people in the hotel. Before he died he asked
the master of the house to do all he could to
facilitate the journey of the child to England,
and, if necessary, to apply for the aid of the
British Minister. He spoke also warmly of the
two servants, saying he had given them full
instructions and letters to his family, and that
they were to take the child to England, and
also his money and his luggage.

"At the steamboat office I was told that
they knew nothing of Blaine. He had, as
stated by the nurse, taken passages to Southampton for himself, the nurse, and the child,
by the Britannia, which sailed from Lisbon on
27th January; and they heard afterwards, at
the office, that he had missed the ship. Since
that time they have not seen him.

"Then I addressed myself to the police,
and obtained, through the kind intervention
of the Consul, permission to examine the daily
reports from and after the 27th January, the
day on which Blaine returned ashore from the
steamer. No one in any way like him had
come to any inn or lodging-house in Lisbon, or
had been received into the hospitals. Nor

could I discover any trace of him at any of
the shipping or diligence offices.

"Finally, I asked for the list of accidents
and suicides, and I regret to say it seems not
impossible that this may have led me to a clue.

"On the 2d of February, the body of a man
was found floating in the Tagus, with two
stabs in the chest. The man had been dead
apparently four or five days. He had no
clothes on but his trousers. As his skin was
white and his hair fair, it was supposed he
was a foreigner. There was an old scar, as if
from a sword-cut, on his left shoulder. The
body, which was much decomposed, was buried
immediately by the police, who seem to have
made no inquiries about the man, being accustomed, apparently, to find bodies in the Tagus.

"The idea that the body might perhaps be
that of Blaine, induced me to inquire of the
porter and the waiters at the hotel, whether
they knew anything of his habits during the
time he passed in Lisbon, or of the persons,
if any, whom he frequented. I was informed
that he often went out alone in the evening,
after his master had gone to bed, and returned
usually rather late. No one knew, however,

where he went, excepting that it was down the
hill towards the river. It occurred to me that,
as Blaine could not speak Portuguese, it was
improbable he would have made acquaintances,
unless it were amongst the few seafaring English who are to be found in small boarding-
houses or drinking - places along the Tagus.
So I visited all the houses of that description
which are known to the Consul or the police;
but I could learn nothing. It may be pre-
sumed that the motive which brought Blaine
ashore again from the Britannia had, in all
probability, some connection with the visits he
was in the habit of making at nights; but, on
all that part of the case, I have failed thus far
to discover anything. I can only suppose that
he did not mean to remain on shore, and that
on the contrary it was his intention to return
to the steamer, for he had taken his own luggage on board with the nurse, and had left
it there.

"A detail of considerable interest, which
was mentioned to me by one of the waiters,
is that Blaine stated to him, after the Colonel's
death, in the presence of other persons, that
he had the Colonel's money upon him to con-

vey to England, and that he did not like the responsibility of carrying it about. Such a fact, if known, would be of a nature to induce robbers to lay a trap for him.

"It would be premature to say that the body found in the Tagus on the 2d February was that of Henry Blaine. To assist in deciding that question, we have at our disposal two possibilities of identification. The first is the scar on the left shoulder. Had he such a scar? His family (if you could find them) could probably inform you upon that. The trousers offer the second chance. I have succeeded in obtaining them from the police, and have shown them to the people of the hotel, but no one there could recognise them. I shall bring them with me to England, in the hope that the nurse may be able to say whether she has seen them worn by Blaine. They are discoloured, stained, and torn.

"I shall remain here a few days longer to continue my inquiries, and expect to be able to return by the next steamer.

"In conclusion, I ought to observe that the nurse's story, so far as you have related it

to me, seems to be fully corroborated by all
I have learnt here.—I am, Sir, your faithful
servant,   C. GRAY."

When Miss Brandon had finished reading
this letter (which Mr Cumber brought to her
directly it arrived), she sat back in her chair,
closed her eyes, and remained silent. Even
her nature, with all its sturdiness, was crushed
for a moment by the news. After a time,
she said, with a broken voice, "But if Blaine
is murdered and robbed, the letter must be
lost."

Mr Cumber replied, "It would be going too
far to admit at once that the body found
in the Tagus was that of Blaine. But the
delay in his arrival here, combined with the
impossibility of tracing him at Lisbon, does
certainly point to the hypothesis that he may
have been murdered. In that case there can
be little doubt that whatever he had upon
him, money or papers, would be taken ; and
if the letter from Colonel Brandon to the
General were in his pocket, it would, in all
probability, be stolen with the rest."

"If it were in his pocket?" interrupted Miss

Brandon, waking up again. "Where could it be, excepting in his pocket? It was not in his luggage; we know that. Therefore it was in his pocket. That is certain."

"Not certain; only very likely," answered Mr Cumber, gently. "I fear, however, that, wherever it was, it has disappeared, and I do not yet see any plan by which we could hope to get it back again. If Blaine was drawn into some low hole in Lisbon, and killed there for the money he was known to have upon him, we must suppose that the murderers would destroy everything that could compromise them, and a letter would certainly be burnt. It cannot therefore be reasonably expected that we should gain anything by offering a reward for the recovery of the letter. Still, we could make the attempt, provided we could obtain immunity from the Portuguese authorities for the person who restored it. But we need not think of that for the moment. We must, first of all, try to discover whether the body was really that of Blaine. His mother ought to know about the scar. Most luckily I have her address in that letter from her which we found in Blaine's

boxes. It is somewhere in Somersetshire. I
will write to her at once. And I should like
to ask a question of the nurse; would you be
so kind as to have her called, and to interpret
for me?"

When Berthe came in, Mr Cumber said to
her, " Have you any recollection of the clothes
that Henry Blaine used to wear?"

" Oh yes. He had very few clothes. So
far as I know, he had only two suits besides
his black clothes; one was all grey, and the
other was a black jacket and waistcoat and
brown trousers."

" Can you remember which of the two suits
he wore on the day you embarked on board
the Britannia at Lisbon?"

" He wore the grey suit. He told me he
had packed up the other, which was the better
one of the two, and that the grey was all
he wanted for the voyage. And I know it,
too, for another reason. After the luggage had
gone away from the hotel to the steamer,
Henry stooped to pick up something, and
the button that held his brace came off. He
asked me to sew it on again for him, and
I did. I laid the baby on the bed, and I sat

upon a chair, and he stood before me. And as my sewing things were in my box, I had no black thread—I remember that because we talked about it; and I sewed the button with white thread I had in my pocket in this,"— and she took out of her pocket a little wooden cotton and needle case such as many French servants have.

"On which side of his trousers did you sew the button?"

"On the left side."

"Well," said Mr Cumber, as soon as Berthe had quitted the room, "this curious detail may clear up the question. How very singular the composition of evidence often is! In this case we have the scar as well; but if there had been no scar, the proof might have depended on the colour of the thread that sewed that button. We shall see when Mr Gray brings the trousers. But we can get quicker information from Blaine's mother. If she says her son really had the scar, and if the trousers are grey, with a button on the left side sewn with white thread, there will, I fear, be no room for doubt."

And then Miss Brandon broke in with a

trembling voice,—" But, Mr Cumber, what are we to say—what can we say—to my brother George ?"

" The truth, my dear Miss Brandon—the truth, as I have already answered you on a previous occasion. There is nothing to be hidden, and your brother has a right to know all. You expected Blaine to arrive, and to bring the legal evidence of the Colonel's marriage. It appears probable, unhappily, that Blaine has disappeared, and that the evidence sent has disappeared with him. We must say so to Mr George Brandon."

" If so, Mr Cumber," went on Harriet Brandon, with more energy, " surely you can add that we shall take immediate steps to obtain the evidence from other sources. The marriage must have taken place in France. I cannot doubt that we shall find the proofs of it."

" Well, it may have been performed in France," replied Mr Cumber, with his usual prudence ; " we do not know with any certainty. As the lady was French, and as the nurse heard that she died in France, there is some justification for supposing that she was married there. But remember, that is

only a presumption. Still, if we could get
hold of any facts to work upon, we might
employ detectives. I suppose we shall be
able to find out where the Colonel stayed
in France, and in that way we shall obtain
the first clues to follow. It is late, and I
must leave you now ; I do not want to lose
a post in writing to Blaine's mother. To-
morrow I will send a copy of Gray's report
to Mr George Brandon."

When Mr Cumber had gone, Miss Brandon
went up-stairs to the child and sat down by
its side. It was asleep. She watched it with
an agitation which nothing in her experience of excitability, large as it was, had at all
prepared her for. In her previous vehemen-
cies she had always recognised that, whatever were their causes, they were merely
temporary, and would expire of themselves.
She had even told herself sometimes that
it was very unsatisfactory, and even rather
ridiculous, to indulge so often in emotions
which by their nature were destined to wear
out so fast. Yet she had gone on with them
—in part by habit, in part because she had
nothing else to put in their place, and because

losing her temper was a convenient and easily
attainable form of ardour. But now she felt
she had within her a new and very different
source of sensation—one that would require
no renewal, and would last, unexhausted, because it sprang from truth and love. She
whispered as she watched—" My child, my
darling! you have altered my whole existence. You have opened up a new life to
me. Until you came, I was good for nothing; now I have an object and a duty. And
you, sweet little innocent, the cause of this
change in me, sleep there in ignorance of
all you have done to me — of all that is
happening about yourself, of the grave interests which your appearance has set in
action. You have fallen here to brighten and
to occupy my uselessness, and to show me
that I can love; and perhaps, sweet child,
you have fallen here to suffer. But the good
that you have done in teaching me that I can
feel and act, shall be repaid by me to you in
love and gratitude. Through you, poor baby, I
have learnt in a few weeks much more about
myself than I ever knew before. I am beginning to have an involuntary respect for

myself that is absolutely new to me. But,
darling, it is not a respect that gives me
vanity; it grows from a very different root—
from the sentiment of utility and duty. How
could I have lived to my age without an
object? I see that now; and I wonder. But
yet I did live, in spite of the utter emptiness
of my heart. That shows how unconscious
we are of our uselessness—until we learn to
be useful; then only do we become able to
measure rightly our previous condition. I
should like to know whether other lonely
women would feel under similar circumstances
just what I feel, or whether the sensations of
others would take different shapes from mine.
It is indeed most glorious to feel — to feel
supremely, permanently, I mean; to feel with
the unspeakably satisfying certainty that I
shall go on feeling unchangeably, unweaken-
ingly, for life. I used to think I felt sometimes—when I did my dry duty to the village people, and saw that I was rendering
service, and that they were pleased. As if
that were feeling! Oh no! there can be
no real feeling without love, and I suspect
that even love would not create complete feel-

ing unless combat were annexed to it—as in
my case. At least my nature seems to tell
me that."

And then the baby woke, and stretched out
its arms to her and pulled her. And there
was a scene of tenderness which made Miss
Brandon recognise once more that she was
changed.

Two days afterwards Mr Cumber brought
out to her another letter from Mr George
Brandon. It said :—

"LONDON, 6th April 1862.

"MY DEAR CUMBER,—I have received your
letter of yesterday, enclosing a copy of a report addressed to you from Lisbon by Mr
Gray.

"I learn from that report — firstly, that
proof has been obtained of the death of my
brother; secondly, that the servant said to
have been intrusted by my brother with the
papers attesting his supposed marriage has
disappeared.

"Under these circumstances, I shall be glad
to hear whether you have any grounds for
imagining that the evidence you talk of seek-

ing elsewhere is likely to be obtained within any reasonable period.

"I should regret to take any steps which might cause pain to my sister, who appears to believe the story of my brother's marriage, and to admit the legitimacy of the child who was brought so strangely to Hurley on the 2d February. But you will understand, I am sure, that I cannot allow my own rights, as heir - at - law of my uncle and brother, to remain indefinitely in suspense. — Sincerely yours, GEORGE BRANDON."

CHAPTER III.

"WELL, this time George speaks out," said Miss Brandon excitedly to Mr Cumber, when she had read her brother's letter. "He denies that Charles was married, and he claims Hurley for himself. That is what his letter comes to, and that is how he respects the wishes expressed by Charles on his deathbed. What an admirable brother he is! What an example of goodness and affection he sets us! I have always mistrusted him, yet I never imagined he could behave in this fashion to his own family. We will fight him to the end, Mr Cumber; and, please God, we will beat him! But the duty I have to discharge to Charles and to his child has roused in me a feeling of liability I never had before. I see that this time it will not be sufficient to lose my temper in order to have my own way. I know I am headstrong, but I know also that the law is even more self-willed than I am, and now that I may have to go to law for others and not for myself, I mean for the first time to be extremely calm and extremely prudent. So tell me, please, what is the law?"

Mr Cumber answered, "It is not easy to foresee with certainty how a court or a jury would judge a case of this kind. I think, however, it must be considered probable that if Mr George Brandon takes proceedings to dispute the rights of the child, she would not, under all the circumstances, be regarded as legitimate, in the legal sense of the word, unless we can produce material evidence of the marriage."

"Mr Cumber, how can you say so?" broke in Miss Brandon, unable to restrain herself, and forgetting all her promises of moderation. "To imply that Claire may perhaps be disinherited is to shock me to the very bottom of my heart. If that is what you have to tell me, I do not want to hear it."

"My dear lady," was Mr Cumber's reply, " you asked me for my opinion as a lawyer,

not as a man. Permit me, I entreat you, to
speak to you as a lawyer, and, whatever I
may be forced to say in that capacity, do not
doubt my friendship or my sympathy. Per-
sonally, I am as convinced as you are that
your brother Charles was married, and that
this is his lawful daughter; but my personal
conviction is a very different thing from legal
proof. And, furthermore, I am bound to
point out to you that my position as trustee
under the will imposes on me responsibilities
of a special kind. I have to see—I trust you
will permit me to say it without offending
you — that the law of inheritance is obeyed;
and even if the marriage were not disputed by
Mr George Brandon, it might be my duty to
ascertain, under the singular circumstances
which have arisen, who is legally the heir-at-
law and the next of kin of General Brandon. If
this child is, as I am sure she is, the legitimate
daughter of Colonel Charles Brandon, then she
is both his heir-at-law and next of kin, and in
those two capacities inherits Hurley and the
personal property as well, in virtue of the
terms of the General's will bequeathing everything to her father, or, failing him, to her

father's heir.   But, if the marriage of her
parents cannot be legally proved, then your
brother George becomes the heir-at-law, and he
and yourself conjointly are the next of kin, in
which case Mr George would get Hurley ; the
personalty, after the legacy to yourself, would
be divided equally between him and you, and
the child would get nothing.   She would not
even inherit Colonel Charles Brandon's personal
property (supposing him to have made no
will).   That also would be divided between Mr
George and yourself.   You see, therefore, that
the course pursued by your brother introduces
in reality very little change into the nature of
the difficulties before us.   If he were animated
by a friendly spirit, an arrangement might
perhaps be effected as regards the disposal of
the property ; but no arrangement, however
friendly, could, if we are unable to obtain
evidence of the marriage, bestow on this little
child the legal status of her father's heir."

" But Charles's letter, Mr Cumber !" exclaimed Miss Brandon, who had been listening
to this statement with scarcely controllable
impatience.   " Does Charles's own letter count
for nothing ?   Is his own signed declaration

that he was married, and that Claire is his child, valueless in the eyes of the law ?"

" It would count, I am convinced, for something," was the reply. "It is conclusive evidence to you and me. It would be moral evidence to the world at large. Even the law would look at it, I fully believe, with a certain confidence and sympathy. But remember that it was not written by your brother—it is only signed by him ; and as the man who wrote it is in all probability dead, we can produce, I fear, no proof about it. The law, if we have to resort to it, will not content itself with the testimony of that letter—it will claim certificates and attestations—it will call for witnesses ; and if no such evidence can be produced, the law will harden its heart and say there is no proof. So when you ask me what the law is, I am obliged to tell you that I do not think the child will be regarded as legitimate in law if we fail to show, in the form required, when and where the marriage was performed."

" But we are going to find out the when and the where !" exclaimed Miss Brandon.

"We are going to *try* to find it out," responded Mr Cumber, "and I trust we shall succeed. That is all we can venture to say for the moment."

"And if we do not find it out?" asked Miss Brandon, gloomily.

"Ah, in that event, I fear the child will be declared to have no legal rights at all. Even the name of Brandon would not properly belong to her."

"Good God!" cried Miss Brandon, springing to her feet and throwing up her hands in horror. "The child would have no right to her father's name?"

"But if the law refuses to admit that she is her father's child?" replied Mr Cumber.

"Oh, Claire, my darling, my poor darling!" gasped Miss Brandon, breaking into sobs in her distress. "And Charlie too, my dear Charlie, how little you foresaw this! What a scoundrel George is!"

"No, Miss Brandon, no. Permit me to assure you that Mr George is not at all a scoundrel for acting as he does. His letter to me is moderate in form; he implies that he is ready to give us time to seek for evidence. I really do not think—if you will allow me to say so—that, taking human nature as it is, and considering what men will do for money, he is to blame for putting in his claim. The circumstances are peculiar. You must not forget, in your emotion, that your uncle meant Mr George to have the property, and that he told me to prepare a new will to that effect. Morally, therefore, Mr George is fully justified in considering himself to be the proper heir. And as regards the child, the absence of legal proof (if we fail to obtain it) would leave her in a very unsatisfactory position. I spoke just now of a friendly arrangement——"

" No, no, Mr Cumber, I will have no friendly arrangement," interrupted Miss Brandon, with all her old violence. "I will have no friendly arrangement at all. Either George will recognise and act upon the dying wishes of his brother, as they are expressed in Charlie's letter to me, or he will dispute them, in which case I will consent to no arrangement. The child either is or is not Charlie's child, born in wedlock; if George says it is not, I will fight him to the last. And furthermore, Mr Cumber, it is not true that he has any moral rights; it is not true

that my uncle really meant him to have Hurley. He told you he would leave it to him,
because he fancied it was right, in principle,
to do so, and because, when he consulted you
about it, you made no objection ; but when he
came back that day from Lorston, after seeing you—the day he died—he told me he was
disgusted at having to do it, and that in his
heart he did not wish George to inherit the
estate. So, Mr Cumber, do not talk to me
about my uncle's intentions ; I know more
about them than you do. No, Mr Cumber,
George has no rights at all, either moral or
legal, and we will fight him and beat him."

" But, my dear lady," answered Mr Cumber,
increasing his softness of tone in proportion to
the growing asperity of Miss Brandon's language, " it is not possible to fight without
weapons. If we have no arms in our hands,
we can only claw and scratch, we cannot fight.
And you must let me remind you that, thus
far, we have no arms."

" We will find them, Mr Cumber ; we will
forge them by force of will and energy. We
will hunt all over France, and we will trace
the marriage. We know the date, approxi-

mately. We will put advertisements into the
newspapers. We will offer rewards for information. We will employ detectives—you said
so yourself. We will follow Charles from place
to place. We will search out his acquaintances. Charles's honour and Charles's truth
are at stake, as well as the name and the position of his child. Charles has said that he was
married, and it is our duty to prove it, Mr
Cumber."

And Miss Brandon stopped, out of breath,
having poured out all these declarations in
one burst.

"Of course, of course," answered Mr Cumber, "we will do all this and as much more
as we can. But we must suppose that as
Colonel Charles Brandon intended to conceal
his marriage, he took all possible precautions
to surround it with secrecy, and that we shall
have in that fact (if, as I expect, it is a fact)
an obstacle the more to vanquish. The whole
case presents—I cannot conceal my opinion—
an appearance of growing difficulty and uncertainty, and it is my duty to point out to you
that I do not regard success as assured. We
need proof, not only of the marriage, but of

the child's birth as well; evidence of the first would be of little use without evidence of the second, so our task is double. Considering everything, considering especially the gravity of the consequences of failure, it is my duty to suggest to you that, notwithstanding what you said just now, a friendly arrangement with Mr George Brandon, on the basis of the second will which your uncle gave me verbal instructions to prepare (although you say he regretted he had done so), would get over the more serious of our difficulties; for, of course, the condition of it would be that the child's birth should not be publicly disputed. Having now laid my views before you, I leave you to decide. The power of decision is clearly yours. Colonel Brandon has placed his child in your hands, by his letter to you, and you have, therefore, the right to act as what is called the child's 'next friend'—that is to say, its representative before the law."

"I accept that position and that responsibility," replied Miss Brandon, with sudden calm and deep earnestness. "Nothing could be clearer from my standpoint than the duty I have to perform, and I will listen to no compromises. My brother, on his deathbed, confided his child to me, telling me at the same time of his marriage. I accept the charge, as a whole, with all its meanings and all its consequences. The first of its meanings is, that Claire is the lawful child of Charles. The first of its consequences is, that I have to get the child recognised in that quality. I can admit nothing else; I can think of nothing else. Besides, I feel within me that we shall obtain the proofs. The extraordinary disappearance of Henry Blaine and the consequent loss of the papers he was bringing, have created difficulties which no one could have foreseen; but my nature does not permit me to doubt that difficulties, whatever they be, can be vanquished by effort and perseverance. My heart too, as well as my will, is bent upon success. I love Claire with my whole soul, and it is impossible for me to suppose that, in such a case, a case in which my brother's honour and his daughter's name are at stake, fate will have the injustice, the cruelty, to decide against us. Therefore, Mr Cumber, with all deference to your opinion, and with warm thanks to you for giving it to me, we

will maintain our position as it is. We will
claim for Claire her rights, her entire rights, as
daughter and heir of Colonel Charles Brandon
—which she is."

Mr Cumber reflected for some moments,
and then said, with a good deal of gravity,
" The decision you have adopted places me
in a very painful situation. So long as you
had not declared definitively that you will
resist Mr George Brandon's claim, if he makes
one, it was unnecessary for me to say what I
am now about to say ; and as all my sympathies
are with you, and as I am as anxious as yourself to obtain proofs of the marriage, I have
worked on with you up to the present. But
after what you have just said, I am bound to
point out to you that, whatever be my feelings
as your old personal friend, I may be forced,
in my capacity of trustee of your uncle's will,
to take up an attitude which might not be
identical with—which might, indeed, be in
opposition to—your own. As trustee of the
will, I am bound to retain entire liberty of
action, and it would neither be delicate nor
right for me to act as solicitor for a litigant
with reference to a will of which I am

myself the trustee. Consequently, my dear Miss Brandon, I am now obliged, with infinite regret, after what you have just said, to ask you to choose another adviser for the purposes you have in view. I will do everything I can to aid you to discover the truth—it is my duty to do so; I most earnestly hope you will succeed; but now that you have decided, finally, that you will fight the case, I cannot continue, technically, to act for you. It would be altogether irregular and improper for me to do so."

This sudden and unexpected declaration paralysed Miss Brandon. She stared at Mr Cumber as if she did not understand him; she remained for a minute motionless; it was evident that the blow had stunned her. When she began to rally, she pressed her hand to her head, then she looked vaguely round her, and at last, in a low voice and with much effort, she said, " Mr Cumber, I respect your scruples. To a certain extent, even, I comprehend them. But to lose your professional aid is, in my position, a most cruel addition to my cares. Tell me, at all events, what I had better do. Without you, as with you, I go on with the

battle ; but tell me—I suppose you can do so
without impropriety—to whom can I confide
the case ?"

" I was on the point of suggesting to you
to select my London agent, Mr Holmes; he
is a very safe man, and I recommend him
strongly to you.   And for anything you may
need here, Mr Gray — who will, no doubt, be
back immediately—can act for you on account
of Mr Holmes.   All that it may be possible to
do myself shall be done.   I beg you not to
doubt that."

And then Mr Cumber left, and Miss Brandon went to the child's room, and took her
in her arms, and looked at her wistfully and
sadly, and tried to smile and talk to her, but
could not.

The next morning Mr Cumber sent out
word that an answer had arrived from Mrs
Blaine, stating that her son Henry had on his
left shoulder the scar of a sabre-cut he had received in India when he was a soldier there.

In the afternoon of the same day Mr Gray
returned to Lorston.   Mr Cumber came with
him at once to Miss Brandon's cottage, and
the trousers he had brought from Lisbon were

examined. They were grey, and the brace button on the left side of the waistband was sewn with thread which, though discoloured and darkened by soaking in dirty water, was almost white in comparison with that which held the other buttons. The nurse immediately recognised the trousers, notwithstanding their stained condition, and declared unhesitatingly that the button was the one sewn on by her before she had embarked at Lisbon.

"There is now no room for doubt," said Miss Brandon. "The double proof of the scar and the button is decisive. It was Henry Blaine. The letter is gone."

And then there was a silence. After a while Mr Cumber said, " As we drove here, I have talked over with Mr Gray the details of his report. He discovered nothing more during his last week in Lisbon, and I fear we must regard that part of the subject as exhausted. The idea of offering a reward for the recovery of the letter occurred to Mr Gray, and he inquired what could be done in that direction. Unfortunately, he found that, in addition to the ordinary improbabilities that such a course would produce any result, it would be rendered substantially impracticable by the unwillingness shown to him by the Portuguese authorities to promise a pardon to any person who might bring the letter. We must now take it as a fact that the papers which Blaine was to deliver to General Brandon have disappeared. You have decided, Miss Brandon, to seek elsewhere for evidence of the marriage and of the child's birth. Would you like Mr Holmes to come down here to talk the matter over, and to receive your instructions ? "

" Certainly ; if you please. And I should like my uncle's papers to be looked through carefully, in order to be quite sure that no letters from Charles are amongst them. I know my uncle never kept letters ; but sometimes, by accident, they escape destruction ; and it is so essential to trace the places from whence Charles wrote, that it will be prudent to make a complete examination. I think, too, we ought to see whether Mrs Blaine possesses any letters from her son. Where Charles was, Henry Blaine was ; so places mentioned by the latter would put us on the track of the former. Besides, it is our duty to break to

Mrs Blaine the news of her son's death. I suggest, therefore, if you have no objection, that Mr Gray should go to Mrs Blaine for the double purpose of acquainting her with what has happened, and of inquiring about the letters."

"I quite agree with you," said Mr Cumber. " I have already examined your uncle's papers, but I will go through them again, and I will write to Mr Holmes to come as soon as he can. Mr Gray shall go to-morrow to Somersetshire to see Mrs Blaine."

The search through General Brandon's papers produced no results at all ; not one single letter from anybody was found.

But Mr Gray was more successful ; he brought back with him eight letters from Henry Blaine to his mother, which, with their envelopes, she had carefully preserved. These letters were of various dates, extending from 1859 to the end of 1861. They came successively from Rouen, Biarritz, Versailles, and Lisbon. The first four of them were from Rouen, and were dated May and November 1859, and January and April 1860. As the marriage was known to have taken

place somewhere about the first of those
four dates, and the death of Mrs Brandon
about the last of them, it seemed not unreasonable to infer that the marriage and the
death occurred in Rouen or its neighbourhood.
The letters themselves contained nothing of
the faintest interest; they were very short,
and made no allusion to events or plans.
There was, indeed, an appearance of studied
reticence about them which confirmed the
idea previously expressed by Mr Cumber that
Colonel Brandon (and consequently Blaine)
had tried to conceal his movements. And
there was a peculiarity about the four letters
from Rouen which gave force to this presumption. While the letters from Biarritz, Versailles, and Lisbon—written after Mrs Brandon's death—mentioned, as if there were
nothing to conceal, the hotel at which Blaine
was staying at each of those places, the
letters from Rouen gave only Poste Restante
as the address to which his mother was to
send her answers. This indication, repeated
four times from the same place during a whole
year, could not have been due to any temporary uncertainty of abode; it was mani-

festly intentional, and, under the circumstances, the intention could only be to conceal the name of the hotel or house where
Colonel Brandon lived.

These considerations seemed to point so
distinctly to Rouen, or some village round it,
as the Colonel's probable place of residence,
at the moment of his marriage and during
the life of his wife, that Miss Brandon's heart
leaped with joy, and she cried out, " We have
found it ! "

Mr Cumber and Mr Gray agreed that the
evidence supplied by these letters seemed to
justify the hope that they had obtained a clue.

As soon as they had left, Miss Brandon, in
the fulness of her suddenly born confidence
and hope, sat down and thought. It was a
most unusual act for her to think by herself,
as other people do. Her habitual way of
thinking was to pour out a monologue to
some one else ; but this time she felt it would
be a desecration of her dreams to tell them
aloud. Fancies which seemed to her almost
holy had rushed into her since she had found
herself able to believe, a few minutes before,
that she had got on to a track at last. To

her emotional nature success seemed, for the
moment, certain. Doubt disappeared. She
floated on a bright sea of hope. Eagerly,
delightedly, in the intensity of her longing
to discharge what she considered to be her
mission, in the effusion of her duty towards
her brother, and of her fervent love for his
child, she dreamed a daylight dream. A fit
of intoxicating motherhood came over her.
The life of Claire appeared before her. She
imagined she was installed with her at Hurley
Park. She thought of the prodigious education she would give her; of the means she
would employ to bring her into contact with
all the forms of knowledge, skill, and grace.
She should be taught what no girl had ever
learnt before, and be taught without effort,
by mere absorption. And then she thought
of her grown into a young woman, all beauty,
intelligence, and charm, possessing all capacities, all aptitudes, all fascinations. She
thought of the effect she would produce, of
the admiration she would excite, of the con-
test between men to win her. She thought
of her as wife and mother, superb in person,
matchless in conduct, apart in wisdom, courted,

loved, and honoured. And in her vision she saw in Claire the outcome of her own guidance, of her own efforts to produce a perfect woman, and she rejoiced in the future of her work. Her nature overflowed with the imagination of triumphant maternity. She decided that she would be the most successful mother the world had ever known. She had not, for the instant, one doubt of her capacity to be so. She had, indeed, made progress since the day, a few months before, when she had looked with terror at the mission thrust upon her, and had told herself she was incapable to fulfil it.

And as she dreamed all this, the nurse brought Claire in from the garden, and the child, who was beginning to speak, held out her arms and called Miss Brandon "Tatte," which was her way of pronouncing Tante. And the dream faded away and was replaced by a sweet reality of tenderness. That afternoon the cottage was full of momentary happiness, and trust, and fondness. Berthe had her full share of it, for events had brought her into such close and special contact with Miss Brandon, that sorrows and joys about the child were beginning to be almost in common between them; and as the nurse was a good woman and fairly intelligent as well, her new mistress had found it natural to extend to her some part of the interest she felt about the child.

The next day Mr Holmes came down from London. The case was explained to him in all its details. He took it up with warmth, thought there was no room for reasonable doubt that the marriage had really been performed somewhere in the neighbourhood of Rouen, expressed hopes of success, and returned to town to choose a detective and send him off at once.

For some while after this Miss Brandon remained in the state of delighted trust into which she had been thrown by the finding of the Rouen clue. She passed the hours in eager waiting for the arrival of the expected proofs, in thought of the arrangements to be carried out so soon as all was settled, and in tender dreamy playing with the child. All violence was gone from her.

Yet, discovery did not come.

Mr Holmes wrote frequently, reported that

the detective was actively at work ; but added always that, so far, he had unravelled nothing.

Day followed day ; letter followed letter. Delay made Miss Brandon impatient, nervous, apprehensive. Hope lessened ; disquietude increased, and, by degrees, the conditions of biting anxiety and suspense through which she had already passed, while waiting for Mr Gray's report from Lisbon, grew up once more. This time, indeed, the strain upon her was even greater than before, for she had borne so much emotion, that she had become, at last, distinctly timid. She, who had always been fearless and resolute, had grown, under the pressure of the new cares that had fallen on her, restless, diffident, and sometimes even frightened. The very ardour of her affection for Claire, instead of bringing her calm, contributed, on the contrary, to augment her disquietude, for it awakened in her a throbbing sense of responsibility, and kept her in an almost unceasing consciousness that she, and she alone, was accountable for the future of the child. All dreams had disappeared ; hope had almost vanished too ; the hard truth alone remained.

In this condition, sometimes despairing,
sometimes in stubborn confidence, she waited
for good news.

But there was no good news.

The detective kept Mr Holmes informed of
all he did ; but of practical results there were
none.   Not a trace of Colonel Brandon, or of
anybody resembling him, could be discovered
in Rouen.   The advertisements inserted in the
local papers brought no replies.   Weeks passed.
The clue that had appeared so guiding had
led to nothing.   It seemed as if the precautions supposed to have been taken by Colonel
Brandon in order to ensure secrecy had been
too complete and too successful.   No information of any kind could be obtained.

Miss Brandon was almost broken down
with disappointment.   She grew silent, even
with the child.

And Mr George Brandon, after writing
several letters to Mr Cumber, inquiring,
pressingly, what his sister meant to do, at
last gave formal notice of his intention to
dispute the legitimacy of the child.

In the midst of this, one morning, the
detective appeared unexpectedly at the cot-

tage and informed Miss Brandon that he had
come to make a verbal report to her on the
position of the case.

He began by delivering a letter from Mr
Holmes informing her that Mr George Brandon had commenced proceedings against the
infant and Mr Cumber as trustee, and that
the trial might be expected to come on at no
distant date. Then, with some emphasis, he
stated that he had been unable to find any
proof whatever of the marriage. All that he
had effected was to collect circumstantial
evidence which seemed to indicate that
Colonel Brandon had made certain prepara-
tions with a view to marrying in France. He
explained that, according to the law of France,
no one, whether he be foreigner or native, can
be married there without producing, firstly,
his own certificate of birth, in order to show
his age; and secondly, either a declaration of
consent to his marriage from his father and
mother, or legal evidence that his father and
mother are dead. The detective went on to
say that, on learning this at Rouen, he had
returned at once to England in order to
consult Mr Holmes as to whether it would

not be advisable to try to ascertain whether
Colonel Brandon had obtained the necessary
papers. It was evident that if he had not
done so, it would be idle to go on imagining
—in the face of the French law—that he
could have been legally married in France;
while if, on the contrary, he really had procured the documents in question, that fact
would furnish very strong presumptive evidence that it was his intention to effect a
marriage in France.

Mr Holmes agreed entirely with this view,
but thought that, under the circumstances,
it would be better to say nothing to Miss
Brandon while the inquiry was going on.
So he wrote, privately, to Mr Cumber, and
was informed by him that Colonel Brandon
had been born at Cheltenham, and that his
father and mother had both died at Brighton.
With these indications to guide him, the detective had succeeded, without much difficulty, in discovering, in each place, the churches
where the child had been christened and the
parents buried. He learnt that, in the month
of February 1859, Colonel Brandon had himself appeared at Cheltenham and at Brighton,

and had asked for copies of the certificates of his own baptism, and of his father's and mother's deaths. There was an unusual circumstance connected with the matter which caused it to be remembered ; the copies, at the particular request of Colonel Brandon, had been signed before a magistrate, the Colonel explaining, though with evident reluctance and hesitation, that he required them for use abroad, and that therefore they needed to be properly legalised.

The detective then went on to say, that as all this had happened only a few weeks before the supposed date of the marriage ; as such documents, expressly authenticated for foreign use, could not be supposed to be required by the Colonel for any ordinary purpose ; and as, on the contrary, they would be indispensable to him in the event of his purposing to marry in France, it seemed reasonable to infer that they were fetched by him in person, in view of the marriage which he wrote afterwards to his sister to say that he had contracted.

The detective finished his story by saying that Mr Holmes had instructed him to come down to Hurley in order to explain the position.

Miss Brandon listened to him with keen disappointment, but, strangely enough, with no desire to interrupt him. Experience was beginning to exercise upon her its usual calming influence, and — sometimes, at all events—it helped her to remain quiet. On this occasion she perceived at once that, however satisfactory it might be to receive additional moral testimony of the probability of the marriage, the fact that the Colonel had fetched the papers supplied no legal proof. Still, she felt comforted by the presumptive evidence obtained by the detective, and, naturally, saw in it an additional motive for persisting in the course she had adopted. Believing, as she did with her whole soul, that the marriage was a reality, it seemed to her that even judges ought to be somewhat influenced by a story in which her brother's letter declaring that he had been married was now supported by the discovery that, shortly before the supposed date of the marriage, he had taken steps which could only be interpreted as meaning that he was preparing to marry. It was in this state of mind that she began to question the detective.

" You say," she said, " that no marriage can take place in France without producing the papers you have mentioned. Do you mean the civil marriage or the religious marriage ?"

" The civil marriage, of course ; the marriage at the Mairie, which is the only marriage that the law recognises. No such papers are required for the religious marriage. But as regards the religious marriage there is something else that I was going to tell you. It appears that no Catholic can be married to a Protestant in a Catholic church without a special dispensation from the bishop of the diocese, and that the dispensation is only granted on condition that all the children shall be brought up as Catholics. Now, as Colonel Brandon was a Protestant, such a dispensation would, of course, have been required in his case ; and as it results from his letter to you that he did pledge himself that the children should be Catholics, I thought I had got on to a new clue, and that if we could find the trace of the dispensation we should in all probability get at the marriage itself. But when I went to inquire at the office of the Archbishop of Rouen, I was informed that no such permission had been applied for. I expressed surprise at this, because I had reason to believe that the marriage had been celebrated in the diocese of Rouen; and it was then suggested, by one of the priests I saw, that perhaps Colonel Brandon had become a Catholic himself, in which case no dispensation would have been required."

"Charles a Roman Catholic!" exclaimed Harriet Brandon. "I do not believe it. And yet, anything is possible. After doing all the rest, he might have done that too. But, to go back to your inquiries, is it possible you have really discovered nothing at Rouen? Have you visited the villages all round? Did my brother hide himself so completely that not a single sign of him can be detected?"

"I have been to every village within twenty miles of Rouen," was the reply. "I have hunted about even at Havre. I have advertised in every paper in the Department. I have put special advertisements for the wet nurse into the Paris papers. I have employed local agents and have offered rewards for information; but I have learnt nothing at all.

If Colonel Brandon really did pass twelve months in or about Rouen, he must have taken very special measures to conceal himself. I have been to Versailles and Biarritz, and have found the hotels where the Colonel stayed with the child and the servants, but that was after his wife's death, and no one there knew anything about her. I have followed the detective business for twenty years, and have had a good many troublesome cases, but I never was so completely beaten as I am this time. I do believe the Colonel meant to marry—what he did about those papers is evidence of that to any reasonable person; but that he absolutely did marry I can't prove yet, and I don't know whether I ever shall."

"You don't know whether you ever shall!" exclaimed Miss Brandon, the old impetuosity rushing up again. "You don't know whether you ever shall! How can a man like you say that? Surely, with your experience, you can suggest further means of action? Surely you are not going to admit that you can do no more? If I were a man I would never acknowledge that I was defeated; I would fight on unceasingly, and be killed rather than give way."

"Then, if you will allow me to say so, ma'am, without offending you," replied the detective, "it is rather fortunate for you that you are not a man, for, according to that, you would be killed a great many times in your life. It seems to me, after a good deal of practice of all this, that it is very useful and very saving of labour to know when to stop; and though it is against my interest to declare that I can't succeed,—because a man like me is always expected to find out something—if not, he doesn't seem to earn his money,—I think we should do well to give this up. You see I have been for two months on the spot, out there at Rouen, and I have been to the bottom of it, and I can't find the bottom, and I don't believe anybody can. There is not a trace of it there, and we have no other clue whatever. I do think the Colonel was married, but he made too good a secret of it, and he has shut the door on us. It was not at Rouen, ma'am; and nobody can guess where else it was."

"But the consequences of failure would be frightful," cried Harriet Brandon, throwing her arms up in horror at the thought. "We *must* succeed. We must go on until we do."

"Oh yes, ma'am, I know that. Mr Holmes told me the whole story, of course, and I know what hangs at the end of it. If you wish to employ anybody else, I will stand out of the way. I should like, professionally, to see the thing found out, because I do believe the Colonel got himself married—somewhere; but, as I said just now, so far as I am concerned, I see no chance left."

When the detective was gone, Harriet Brandon walked up and down the room and meditated, gloomily.

"Give up?" she said to herself. "Give up? I give up? Give up the mission that has been intrusted to me, the duty that has been imposed upon me, the work that has fallen to me to execute? Give up the joy that was opening before me; give up my foremost obligation as a second mother? Give up my promise to Charlie, to the child, to myself? Never! Giving up means all that, and, furthermore, for me to give up would mean that I doubt. Others may doubt—I fear they will—but I? To me the certainty is utter; and to give up would imply that I feel no certainty. It would be an eternal shame to me to give up. I could not look Claire in the face again if I did. Her place in life, her name, her honour, are in my hands. Never will I give up defending them. Charlie, I will do my duty to you and to your child, and you shall be content with me."

And she sat down, resolutely, and wrote to Mr Holmes and to Mr Cumber, and told them both that defeat in an action would, in her eyes, be more honourable than voluntary retreat; that nothing would make her yield, and that she would go on to the end, whatever the end might be.

CHAPTER IV.

TIME passed. The trial was approaching. Harriet Brandon, in spite of her certainty, in spite of her character — perhaps, indeed, by natural reaction from her certainty and her character—was growing nervous. She could neither eat nor sleep. A new anxiety, even more wearing than the others, had pushed itself into her mind ; she began to ask herself whether, after all, she was acting prudently in continuing to resist. When once this pre-occupation had laid hold of her, she found herself unable to shake it off; it irritated her ; it absorbed her. Morally she had not a doubt ; in principle she was quite positive it was her duty to fight on to the end. Her strong feelings of right and wrong, backed up by her belligerent instincts, made it impossible for her to imagine, even for an instant, that there

could be two roads open to her so far as
conscience and rectitude of conduct were concerned. But, in practice, there were other
considerations to be taken into account. The
situation was not made up exclusively of
principles, or of instincts, or of conscience, or
of right and wrong. There were facts in it
as well, and those facts were nearly all against
her. Both Mr Cumber and Mr Holmes had
given her to understand that, as no evidence
was forthcoming, they disapproved her determination to hold out. She was forced, within
herself, to recognise that the future moral
position of Claire was at stake; that defeat
might mean, for her, the deprivation of infinitely more than money and estate; that
it might entail the loss of name and station
too. And name and station could still perhaps
be saved by giving way!

Harriet Brandon groaned in spirit. She
saw all this more clearly each day. And yet
she could not make up her mind to yield.
Her theory of duty was to accept no compromise in anything; she had applied that
rule to all the small difficulties she had encountered in her dull existence, and thought

she could look back with satisfaction to the results she had so obtained. It seemed to her that she had always won, in the long-run, by standing up, without caring for consequences, for what she had supposed to be right against what she had supposed to be wrong. But she could not conceal from herself that her experience had been confined to little questions in which no serious interests had been involved. In the present case, on the contrary, the issues were momentous, morally as well as materially, and the terrible responsibility she might incur, if she lost the battle, became appallingly distinct. The whole morrow of a helpless, unconscious child was in her hands. The burden of decision seemed awful to her.

Yet still she felt she could not — should not—yield.

Then came revulsion the other way. What was responsibility after all ? Cowards might be afraid of it; but she had never been a coward. She, Harriet Brandon, had feared nothing in the past ; why should she fear now, with one of the noblest causes to defend that ever fell to the charge of man or woman ? No ; her duty evidently was to go straight on.

She oscillated from one impression to another, and could bring herself to no decision.
Sometimes she grew violent, and blamed herself indignantly for a hesitation which she
deemed unworthy of a brave nature. But self-
reproach produced no more effect upon her
than reason did. She went on wavering.

Suddenly, after weeks of vacillation and
suffering, when she was utterly worn out by
agitation, an idea rushed into her head. She
would go and see George himself, point out to
him the wickedness of his conduct, and make
him change it.

In her feverish state this proceeding seemed
to her so natural and so simple that she wondered it had not occurred to her long before.
She did not stop to weigh it. She felt a deep
relief in having invented a plan which would
lead her to immediate action, and her sole
thought was to carry it into execution. In
her sudden eagerness she decided to go up at
once and have the matter out. She packed
up some clothes, drove to Lorston station, and
took the first train to London.

During the journey she endeavoured to prepare a speech to deliver to her brother. But

she was incapable of putting two sentences together. She could not even, so excited was
she, concentrate her thoughts on the interview
she was seeking; they wandered off to other
subjects, and then came bursting back, with
an intolerable jar, to the work before her. Her
head became confused; her emotion, though
continually increasing, grew vague and object-
less, and by the time the train reached town
she scarcely remembered why she had come
there.

She had, however, enough consciousness left
in her to go mechanically to a hotel to leave
her luggage, and then to drive to George
Brandon's house.

She found him at home.

The instant her eyes met his her senses
cleared again. The full perception of her
errand tore back into her brain. The passion
of battle shook her. She felt herself, in one
second, fit to fight a giant. Her strength, her
will, her courage, were suddenly limitless. She
stood up to her full height, threw back her
head defiantly, and said, "You need not look
astonished, George. You know why I have
come here. You know it well enough without

my telling you. Give up this wicked action.
Behave as a brother ought to behave, and join
yourself with me to do our duty to the living
and the dead."

George Brandon, who had placed a chair for
his sister, and had sat down in the supposition
that she would do the same, rose again and
answered, "I presume, Harriet, that your
meaning is to ask me to abandon my uncle's
property to the child you have picked up?"

"The child I have picked up?" repeated
Harriet slowly, with staring eyes and with a
voice of mixed unbelief and horror. • "The
child I have picked up? You say that of
your own brother's daughter? You say that
of the child your own brother sent to my care
from his dying bed? Great God! have you
a heart? You call yourself a Brandon? In
the name of duty, truth, and honour; in the
name of love, of right, of goodness; in the
name of the blood that runs within us both;
in the name of all the Brandons who have
transmitted to us an unsullied memory,—I
summon you to retract those hideous words."

George looked coldly at her, and observed,
with complete self-control, "You are excited,

Harriet. Perhaps it is natural you should be so. But excitement is a bad guide in business, and I do not allow it to affect me. This is a matter of pure business. I do not believe —no, do not interrupt me, if you please, I shall not be long—I do not believe that Charles was married. I do not believe one word of the amazing tale to which it has pleased you to give credence. If I believed it, I should act as you do, and should need no pressure from you to allow this child to take the property. But, I repeat, I do *not* believe it. In my eyes, the story of the marriage has been concocted for a purpose. You have done your utmost to obtain proof of it, and have failed. I have waited till you have failed. You cannot lay before me, after all your researches, one single atom of evidence. Your sole motive for believing is, that you received, with the child, a letter written, avowedly, by a servant who disappeared immediately afterwards, and purporting to be signed by Charles. Did he sign it? and if he signed it, with what motive did he sign it? At the best it is a terribly suspicious affair. That the child was his I am ready to admit as possible—if that is any plea-

sure to you. But that the child was born in
wedlock I utterly deny. In consequence, it
is my intention—my definitive intention and
decision, after waiting for all these months—
to insist on my legal right to the property."

" That is your final answer, George ? "

" That is my final answer."

" No appeal will move you ? "

" No appeal will move me. I have given
you the reason why."

" Well, then, I will go," said Harriet
Brandon, in a broken tone. " I have humbled
myself in coming to you. I thought it was
my duty to point out to you the scandal of
all this, to tell you that you are dragging our
name into the mud, to tell you that you are
robbing an orphan of her rights. I expected to
produce some effect upon you — not by my
words, but by the simple honesty of my cause.
It seems that I have failed. Can nothing
touch you ? Do you mean to tell the world,
in a public trial, that, in your opinion, Charles,
for an unworthy purpose, signed a wilful lie
when he was dying ? How much do you
want ? Take Hurley—take all that comes to
me. I need nothing but the child. It is

money that you are after—money alone. You do not want the truth—but income. What is your price? I give you my share. But leave the child her place in the daylight as her father's daughter. Leave to me and to her, George, a name that has not been stained by the conduct of you — my brother." She trembled, hesitated, made evidently a desperate effort, and then said, "On my knees, I supplicate you." And she knelt down and joined her hands in passionate entreaty.

"I have listened," replied her brother, "to the extremely unpleasant observations you have thought fit to address to me. The only answer—pray get off your knees—the only answer I have to make is that, as I have already told you, I mean to assert my rights as my uncle's heir. If you do not wish, as you say, to drag our name into the mud, you have only to give way yourself, and not defend the action."

"Then nothing will move you? Very good. I leave you. From this moment I cease to be your sister. From this moment I will never speak to you, never forgive you. I will not curse you, because that sort of thing burns a woman's mouth, and because it is not my business to punish you. But punishment will come to you. It is possible— it is even probable, I fear—that you will win your action. But success will bring you no joy, and when the day of retaliation comes— and come it will—then it will be my turn."

She turned her back upon him and went away.

The next morning she was at home again; but she had no memory of her return to the hotel, of the night she had passed through, or of her journey back to Lorston. Her recollection of every detail of the interview was, however, violently distinct; her brother was always present before her; his voice was unceasingly repeating the monstrous words, "the child you have picked up"; she felt herself imploring him on her knees; and, above all, her heart was filled to bursting with a maddening sensation of humiliation. The rest was a blank to her.

She asked mechanically for the child, took it in her arms, looked sadly at it, and tried to think. But thought would not come to her; there was no room for it in her head; its

place was taken by the all-engrossing memory
of the scene she had gone through.

Claire played with her and babbled to her;
but, finding that she got no answers and no
kisses, she did as children usually do under
such conditions.— she slipped away. And
Harriet Brandon scarcely knew that she had
gone.

The hours passed, and brought no calm.
Night came and went. It was not until
the second day that the impression she had
received began to soften down. By degrees
the past became less exclusively absorbing,
and the future reappeared with its menaces.
But those menaces were not so affrighting
as they had been. She perceived, as soon
as she commenced again to look at them,
that they had lost a large proportion of the
gravity they had possessed before she went
to London, and that her brother's tone to
her had put an end to her doubts and hesitations. She told herself, as soon as she
was able to recognise the condition of her
ideas, that she had tried to come to an
arrangement and had failed, and she was
relieved and comforted to think so. It did

not occur to her to consider whether the attempt had been made in a wise or a practical form; it was enough for her that it had been made, and that her brother had rejected her advances. It was now useless to give way. It would be a mere sacrifice of dignity to do so, without any corresponding advantage whatever. The struggle must go on to its end. She had done her best, and could address to herself no more reproaches. Of course the future looked as unsatisfactory as ever; but that was a mere fact, and, to her nature, facts had far less interest than principles. The question of principle was now decided. It was idle to talk of giving way; nothing could be gained by it.

She wrote to Mr Holmes, told him what had happened, and acquainted him with her definitive decision to fight the case whatever might be the consequences. He came down to her a few days afterwards for a final consultation, and then, in sadness but not in too great fear, she awaited the result.

At last the day arrived.

George Brandon's counsel was, naturally,

perfectly aware that there was a nasty side
to his client's case, and that public feeling
might easily become excited against him. He
applied himself, consequently, from the opening of his speech, to diminish, so far as he
could, the moral ugliness of the claim. With
that object, he began by speaking with deep
sympathy and esteem of General Brandon,
Colonel Brandon, and Miss Harriet Brandon.
He described the cruel pain his client felt in
being forced, by the highest considerations of
family duty, to bring such an action as this.
But really he had no option in the matter.
He loudly repudiated all thought of money
interest, and pointed out in touching language
that the mere property was of no import
whatever, compared with the honour of a
name which had been transmitted for five
centuries through an unbroken line. It was
to shield the untarnished repute of that ancient
lineage that he stood before them. The story
was most strange. Every detail of it was
amazing. Colonel Brandon had been abroad
for several years. He was supposed to be
travelling, in part for amusement, in part
for health. No one gave a thought to the

idea that he had a wife. Suddenly it was
announced that he was dead, that he had
married secretly, and that he had left a child.
By a letter purporting to have been signed
by him on his deathbed, he announced his
marriage and confided his child to his sister.
Then came something almost more wonderful
still. The servant who had written that letter, at the Colonel's dictation, disappeared—
disappeared, he must remark, under circumstances of the most extraordinary kind, circumstances which opened the door to grave
suspicions that it was the interest of somebody
to get rid of him—and the papers which were
said to have been intrusted to him, in order
to supply proof of the marriage, disappeared
with him. The result was, that no evidence
of the supposed marriage could be produced.
He was constrained to ask whether there had
been any marriage at all? He was constrained to ask whether those papers had
ever existed? Those were the questions he
submitted to the jury. To say the very least,
those questions were open to most serious
doubts. It was his duty, his most painful
duty—yet, painful as it was, he must discharge

it — to remind the jury that frequent cases
had been known, in which fond fathers had
put forward illegitimate children as having
been born in wedlock ; and, without asserting
—of course, he did not permit himself to
assert, for all was uncertainty in the case—
that Colonel Brandon had been actuated by
that motive, he was obliged to point, though
with infinite regret, to the possibility that
such an intention might have existed. He
was forced to add that, as Colonel Brandon
had avowedly deceived his family with
reference to the existence of his pretended
marriage, so, also, might he have deceived
them about the birthrights of this child.
Under conditions of so exceptional a nature,
was it not an imperious obligation for his
client, as the present male head of the family,
to protect himself from the possible reproach
of having permitted the ancestral estates to
fall into unjustified hands ? Hateful as it
was to him to seem to dispute his brother's
tale — the jury would, he knew, sympathise
earnestly with his distress — he felt, in his
heart, that he had no alternative, in order to
escape responsibility, but to bring the case

before their enlightened judgment. And, in addition to the legal bearings of the matter, its moral aspects also obliged his client to take these proceedings. General Brandon himself —though he saw no reason, during the few hours he remained alive after first hearing of the existence of the child, to doubt the legitimacy of that child—had decided at once that, even if she were legitimate, she ought not to inherit the Hurley property. He therefore instructed his solicitors to prepare a second will leaving the estate to his client; but he died before that second will could be executed. In presence of this intention, his client felt himself to be, morally, the designated heir of General Brandon, just as, legally, he believed himself to be his heir-at-law. This fact supplied an additional motive for this action. Finally, his client had instructed him to express his highest admiration of the conduct of Miss Harriet Brandon, who, with noble devotedness, had thought of nothing but what she conceived to be her duty as a tender sister, and who believed in the marriage of her brother simply because she loved him. Nothing could be more exemplary or more deserving of praise. But Miss Brandon's conduct, perfect as it was, proved nothing. The facts remained unchanged by it. He repeated, there was no proof that Colonel Brandon had been married. The Colonel's own tardy declaration to that effect was unsupported, notwithstanding the efforts Miss Brandon had so energetically made to trace the marriage, by the slightest testimony of any sort. He therefore claimed a verdict for his client, because no other verdict was possible.

When it was the turn of Miss Brandon's counsel to speak, he said : " The marriage of Colonel Brandon is proved by his own letter to his sister. It cannot, thus far, be established otherwise. We admit at once that the other evidence we have obtained is only circumstantial. But our contention is that, under all the circumstances, the letter is sufficient, and merits to be taken as sufficient. Our contention is, that there is in this case something more than mere usual testimony—something other than mere fact—something higher even than the law itself. Our contention is, that the honour of an ancient name—of which my

learned friend, pretending to be unaware that
he is himself attacking it, has ventured to
talk as if it belonged to him—is on our side
only, and that it is for us alone to defend that
honour.   Our contention is, that the truth, the
honesty, the fair fame of Charles Brandon, are
assailed here by his own brother.   Our contention is, that we stand here to represent and
to protect the noblest, the purest, the most
touching of all causes—that we are here to
vindicate the memory of a dead man, and
to obtain from you the declaration that that
dead man's name descends untainted to his
daughter.   For motives which the jury will
appreciate—all I will say is, they are not those
pure and elevated motives which it has pleased
my learned friend to enumerate—the plaintiff
comes here to tell you that his brother signed
a lie when he was dying.   I take it for
granted that he thinks nothing of the kind,
and that he is quite as convinced as we are
that his brother's deathbed letter states the
truth.   But even if he really thought that
letter false, what would be the value of his
opinion?   It would stand alone.   General
Brandon did not doubt the absolute truthful-

ness of that letter. Miss Harriet Brandon
will tell you presently that she is convinced
of its veracity. Charles Brandon was a gallant
soldier. There was no braver or more chival-
rous leader of men. While he lived, no tongue
would have ever dared to say he lied. It has
been reserved for his own brother, now that
he is dead, to prefer, before the world, that
loathsome charge against him. This being the
situation of the case, I think the jury will
agree with me that there is in it something
more than a legal question. When Charles
Brandon saw that his end was coming, he
took every means within his power to place
his marriage beyond doubt. He saw the
grave error he had committed in not confess-
ing it before. He wrote to his uncle with the
details; he sent him the certificates; he confided the letter to a faithful servant, and, by
a lamentable fatality, that servant was assas-
sinated, and that letter lost. Because that
servant is dead, it is argued that the whole
story is a falsehood. But the other letter—
the one I lay before you—tells the tale in
simple, mournful words; and though I can
bring forward little in support of it, I claim

that it alone suffices.   Furthermore, I shall
show that Colonel Brandon came to England,
and procured, in person, the documents which
the French law requires to be deposited at the
Mairie by all persons who intend to marry in
France.   The witnesses I shall call will prove
all this.   I venture to assert that the evidence
I shall produce will, though technically incom-
plete, leave no room for doubt as to the reality
of the marriage.   But, as I observed at the
commencement of my statement, I do not
pretend to stand on purely legal grounds.   I
invoke in favour of a father and a child, one
of whom has left us for ever, while the other
has as yet no power of self-defence, the support
which we owe to the helpless, the aid which is
due to the absent.   I appeal to the hearts of
those who hear me, and I entreat them not
to look at this singular case from the nar-
row standpoint of mathematical demonstration, but to view it with the broad and im-
partial appreciation which we derive from
experience of life and character, to judge
it in all its varied elements, and not as
a mere ordinary application of the habitual
rules of evidence.   I count upon a verdict

in favour of Charles Brandon and his daughter, because no other verdict would be compatible with right feeling, with moral justice, or with honour."

Then the nurse, Mr Gray, and the detective told their stories, and gave their explanations, and after them Miss Brandon entered the witness-box.

Her counsel said to her—"Now tell us, if you please, your opinion on the case."

Harriet Brandon raised her voice almost to a shout, and answered with a dignity and a solemnity which produced a profound impression—"Before God, my conviction is, that my brother Charles signed that letter. Before God, my conviction is, that my brother Charles never told a lie. Before God, my conviction is, that the letter states the truth; that my brother, Charles Brandon, was married in France; that Claire Brandon is his lawful daughter, born in wedlock, and that she is his heir-at-law, and therefore heir to the estate of General Brandon, my uncle."

The effect of this declaration was immense. A thrill ran through the court. There was an instinctive movement of applause.

The summing-up was divided, virtually, into two parts. In the first, the judge pointed out that evidence of the nature usually required was entirely absent. In the second, he spoke with a sympathy and a warmth of Harriet Brandon and the child which left no room for doubt that, if his reason as a lawyer obliged him to take up one position, his feelings as a man led him to adopt another. He left the case to the appreciation of the jury.

The jury remained in consultation for five hours, and the excitement in court, while waiting for the end, was intensely keen. When, at last, the door opened, the silence became breathless. The foreman said, with a marked appearance of constraint and regret—" We find that no legal proof has been laid before us of the marriage of Colonel Charles Brandon."

In giving judgment for the plaintiff, the judge observed that he had not seen a more painful family case.

.　　.　　.　　.　　.　　.

The next day Harriet Brandon returned to Lorston. She went straight from the station to Mr Cumber, and said to him, speaking with effort and fatigue, and in detached phrases, " I wish, first of all, to thank you. You have done your best for me, under difficult circumstances. I shall not forget it.

" I quit the cottage at once. I cannot remain in it as tenant of the new owner of Hurley.

" I shall continue to seek for evidence of the marriage.

" Of course I shall keep you informed of my movements and of all I do.

" Now that you are free to act for me again, I shall be much obliged if you will prepare a will for me to sign, leaving everything I possess to Claire.

" She will bear the name of Brandon. I give it to her."

On reaching home she took the child, looked at her for some moments fixedly, and then said in a low voice, " Darling! My child!"

Those were all the words she spoke, but they meant—" I give you my life."

And then she went to her room, sat down, and thought.

She remained alone for several hours. Her head was calm and clear. She had a complete perception of the terrible realities of the position, but she felt no despair ; on the contrary, she retained her resolution, and looked to the future with some remains of hope. The mission she had to discharge had acquired the character of a religion. She concentrated on it all her force of faith, of will, of duty. The trials she had borne, the responsibility she had faced, the intense application of her whole eager self to the work before her, had softened her most singularly. Her tendency to violence had decreased ; she no longer felt the temptation to explode ; a certain faculty of self-command had grown up within her. Both her power and her need of love had sprung from nothing to immensity.

In one direction, however, she had not progressed ; she remained unreasoning and unreasonable. In her, as in so many women— both good and bad—the deductive faculty was absent. Of course she did not know it ; she imagined indeed, on the contrary, that she was particularly argumentative, and would have been astonished and offended if she had been informed that, as a rule, she was inaccessible to reason, and acted habitually on mere impulse ; that her motives were nearly always

instinctive and independent of calculation.
Even when she thought—and she was beginning to think a good deal — her judgments
were emotional, not logical. Fortunately her
impulses were good and generous, and not
often of a nature to lead her wrong.

It was under the influence of these various
sensations and intuitions that she asked herself what she should do. It was easy to say
that she would leave the cottage, but it was
very difficult to choose another home. The
habits of a life seem simple and natural
enough so long as they run on smoothly. It
often happens, even, that we scarcely recognise their existence until the time comes to
break with them. But then, in their accumu-
lated possession of us, they stand out before
us as cherished tyrants, from whose ruthless
but delightful domination we hate to be set
free.

Harriet Brandon fancied, in her organised
old-maidism, that she would suffer a good deal
from a transformation of her existence. And
yet she could not stop at Hurley.

But reflection about her own wants and
ways occupied her only for a few moments.

Her real preoccupation was to select a resting-place that would fit in with the new exigencies which appeared to her to result from the position of Claire. The instant the verdict was pronounced, a resolution had formed itself in Harriet Brandon's head; that resolution was —Never, never shall Claire know this. She did not stop to ask herself whether such a resolution was either wise or realisable; she gave no thought to the inconveniences and even the dangers which might result from it later on; it sufficed to her that it was in harmony with the present condition of her affections and her impulses. She acted, as she always acted, for the present, and according to the lights of the present. So, as Claire was to know nothing, she must be kept away from contact with all persons who could tell her anything. Now Harriet Brandon had seen the newspapers that morning; she had read in them the reports of the trial and the articles upon it, all full of sympathy for herself; she knew, therefore, that everybody would be talking of it, and she thought, with a feeling of shrinking horror, of the frightful possibility that the child might learn her own history.

She had heard that children's memories are retentive, that young imaginations receive sometimes impressions which time does not efface, and, in her fear, she determined that the sole consideration in her choice of a future home should be the certainty—so far as certainty could be assured by watchfulness—that no stories should reach the ears of Claire, either then or later on. A refuge must be found where Claire would be in safety from the indiscretions of tale-bearers, whether acquaintances or servants.

But this limitation of motives did not facilitate the decision ; on the contrary, it rendered it vastly more difficult than it seemed at first. An abode might be found, perhaps, by seeking, in which old habits could be satisfied, old contacts retained, old prejudices humoured. But what spot on earth was safe from gossip ? Even Harriet Brandon, with all her undoubting ardour, could not blind herself to the uselessness of hunting for so imaginary a place. It was as impossible to discover it as it was easy to wish for it. The utmost that could be hoped for was to lessen the probabilities of peril, to diminish the chances of risk; neither peril nor risk could be suppressed altogether.

When, after long meditation, this certainty had forced itself on her unwilling mind—when she had become convinced that she must content herself with a partial solution of the difficulty, because a complete settlement of it was unattainable—there flashed into her a sudden impulse : she rose from the low chair in which she had been sitting, made two steps forward, raised her arms, looked straight and hard before her, and said aloud, "We will go abroad."

As she always acted instantaneously on her decisions, she rang the bell, ordered that Berthe should be sent up, and said to her, "We go to France in a few days. Get ready. Tell no one. We three go alone."

The next morning she went again to Mr Cumber, communicated her decision to him, signed her will, and gave him power to settle all business on her behalf.

A week later she was in Paris. She stopped there for two days to see a lawyer, and to engage a French detective to pursue the traces of the marriage. And then they went to Biarritz.

CHAPTER V.

SPRING was ending, summer was approaching; the season at Biarritz (which, in those days, was almost limited to August and September) had not begun—the place was empty. Miss Brandon, Claire, and Berthe passed the days before the glorious sea. The child was in strong health, and full of joy. Harriet Brandon was calm. The emotion through which she had just passed had been so excessive that it began immediately to produce, by reaction, its own cure. At first the change was limited simply to sensations. Neither convictions nor will were affected by it. She had a mission, and was going to discharge it. She remained at Biarritz as resolute as she had been at Hurley, but she suffered infinitely less. There were indeed, almost from the day of her arrival, moments when she did not suffer at all. The bitter earnestness of her intentions remained unweakened (at least she thought so), but she consented to be quieter, and to rest. She was forced to recognise that, for her own sake as well as for Claire's, she had acted wisely in quitting England, in breaking with the past, and in seeking new surroundings. The strain to which she had been subjected had been too much for her. She had borne it valiantly, as became her nature; while it lasted she had not permitted it to affect her; but, now that it was over, she felt how much it had exhausted her. She needed repose and change, and she found both at Biarritz. The life there, with its new conditions, its strangenesses and its idlenesses, was, in her wayworn condition, particularly soothing. To her surprise she found scarcely any pain in the rupture of her habits. And, above all, she no longer had either duties or occupations which took her away from Claire; they spent the days together in unceasing talk, and play, and love; and the heart of Harriet Brandon grew filled with sweet rejoicing and unwonted gentleness. Her concentration in the child became so absorbing that at moments she almost thanked fate for having driven them together into the solitude of exile.

They stopped at Biarritz, in tenderness and peace, until July, and then, to avoid the coming crowd, they went to Arcachon.

There, amidst the dreariness of the sand-hills and the pine - trees, Harriet Brandon began to feel a little weary of life in a hotel, and to wish for an established home of some sort. It was, of course, most satisfactory from her main point of view, to possess the freedom of a wanderer, and to use it to avoid chatterers. But wandering provided, after all, no real fulfilment of the object she had set before herself at Hurley. It was good enough as a temporary expedient; it was sufficient for a time; but it was inadmissible as a system. A trial of it during a few months had sufficed to bring its unsatisfactoriness into evidence, and to the warlike heart of Harriet Brandon it had the special demerit of seeming to be a flight and a cowardice. There were even moments of reaction when, in her combativeness, she regretted she had left England, and when she was half tempted to return there. Those moments were, however, rare, and they be-

came more and more rare as time passed on.
Her personal feeling was, that she had done
right (she had a strong tendency to imagine
she had done right), and that feeling led her
to consider the policy of fixing themselves
altogether abroad, at all events for some years.
Besides, the day would soon come when the
education of Claire would have to be commenced; when regular habits, the habits that
are not obtainable at hotels, would have to be
formed and followed, when facilities and con-
veniences of teaching would be needed. For
all these reasons a home would have to be
found somewhere, and soon. Why wait?
Why not enjoy at once the advantages of a
home; why not shelter in it the new happiness that seemed to be dawning on them?

But where was the home to be? In spite
of the whisperings of old habits it could not
be in England, because of the danger there
of betrayal of the secret she had determined
to hide from Claire. But that was all Harriet Brandon knew. The rest was void. Outside England she had no acquaintances; she
had never travelled; she knew nothing of the
Continent; she had no sympathies to satisfy, no

preferences, and no inducements. All Europe was at her disposal, but no spot she had ever heard of either attracted her or repelled her; all places were the same to her, provided only she could keep out rumour.

The problem before her—simple as it may look at first sight—is always difficult to work out, even under the best conditions; but in Harriet Brandon's position it was unsolvable, for not only had she no experience of her own, but she had no one to pilot her, and could apply to no one for an opinion. She could only read descriptions in guide - books, and wonder whether they were true. She stared at the question until it half stupefied her, and finally, after weeks of hesitation, allowed herself, languidly, to be persuaded by the hotel-keeper to take a house where she was. This time there was no impulse in the decision. Indeed it was not a decision at all; it was simply an acquiescence; she stopped at Arcachon for the most negative of all reasons—because she could not make up her mind to go anywhere else. Was it possible that her character was beginning to change?

The house was in the pine woods. It was

large and fairly furnished, but it was lonely and
melancholy. A patch of sand around it was
called a garden, in which some flowers tried to
grow. And yet, despite the sadness, life passed
kindly there. The state of mind into which
Harriet Brandon had drifted at Biarritz became strengthened and confirmed. Beginning
as a temporary and even accidental condition,
it glided slowly into permanence from continued action of the same causes. Solitude and
contented love are powerful producers of new
habits, and new habits and new thoughts gained
strength fast in the villa at Arcachon. Harriet Brandon perceived with astonishment, and
sometimes even with vexation, that the ener-
getic resolutions she had formed after the trial
—resolutions which, at that time, had seemed
to her so unquenchable—were becoming gradually blunted. As she had no provocations to
violence, and as her new surroundings were
soothing and contenting, her temper began to
soften down. The memory of Hurley brought
nothing but pain ; so it was driven off, and by
degrees it weakened. Harriet Brandon had
always lived in the present, and at Arcachon
the present, in its infinite sweetness, became to

her more absorbing than ever. She hated the
past; she feared the future; the passing day
was all she cared to think of. But, naturally,
she had recoils. At certain moments she was
angry with herself for seeming to become luke-
warm; she fancied sometimes that she was
failing in her mission, which was to prove the
marriage and loathe her brother George. Yet,
on the whole, she let herself be human; she
yielded to the quelling influence of time and
to the current of her new life, and became
appeased.

They led an indolent existence. They
strolled about in the forest. They drove
sometimes to the sea, especially in storm
time, and gazed at the great waves breaking,
surging, roaring up the dunes. After a few
months, Miss Brandon made three or four
acquaintances amongst the French people
around her. Her fear of strangers was
diminishing. And after all, it was a little
mournful to know no one. Decidedly her
character was changing.

And Claire played, grew, and ceased to
be a baby.

Meanwhile the settlement of the family

affairs had been completed by Mr Cumber, and he had transferred to Miss Brandon's bankers her share of the personal property left not only by General Brandon, but by Colonel Brandon too. The fortune of the latter (who had made no will) had also to be divided, in consequence of the verdict which disinherited Claire, between George Brandon and his sister. The sums were large. In addition to the £20,000 specially bequeathed to her by her uncle, she came in for half of £70,000 he left in securities, and for half of the £40,000 which had belonged to the Colonel. Consequently, including the £1200 a-year she had previously possessed, she found herself with an income of above £4500. As the utmost she could spend, with her then mode of life, did not exceed £1500, she was, for the moment, needlessly rich. But there was Claire and the future.

The new French detective achieved no more success than his English predecessor. He advertised and searched, but he discovered nothing. Yet, for a long time, Miss Brandon would not consent to give up the pursuit. It was

not until twelve months had been employed
in useless inquiries, accompanied by useless
expenditure, that she consented, on the reiterated advice of both her Paris lawyer and Mr
Cumber, to suspend the investigation.

And then the years passed on ; years of
tender quiet and contentment for Harriet Brandon ; years of health and childish joys for Claire.

Her education had commenced—the education that, in the first fond dreamings of her
aunt, was to make of her a product hitherto
unknown. It began, however, as in other
less ambitious cases, with an alphabet and a
Noah's ark.

One day, when Claire was eight, a reason
came for leaving Arcachon. A Madame
Hoche, who lived in the nearest house, and
who had slowly become a real and earnest
friend, ran in to say excitedly that her son,
who had been French Consul at Pernambuco,
was transferred to Venice, and that she was
going there to him. Thereon, for the first
time for years, Harriet Brandon had an impulse—she would go to Venice too. She had
at last a motive for choosing one place rather
than another, and she leaped upon it. She

told herself that Arcachon without her friend
Madame Hoche, would cease to be Arcachon,
and that Venice with Madame Hoche, would
be more than Arcachon had ever been. So
she transferred her home from the Atlantic to
the Adriatic.

It was at Venice that Claire budded from
a child into a girl. She breathed sunlit air
when her first glimpses into life opened out
before her. Some of the faults and some of
the qualities of the South grafted themselves
on to her nature. Her inborn character was
influenced by the thoughts, the ways, the
words of the race amongst which she had been
brought. At Venice and its neighbourhood,
where she remained for seven years, the basis
of her education was filled in. It was at
Venice that she made her first communion,
an act that remains in the memory of every
Catholic. It was at Venice that she acquired
the consciousness of what music is and can be,
the dawning conception of the uses of art in
daily life. She was pushed exceptionally on-
wards by the nature of her surroundings;
at an age when most other girls are still
struggling with beginnings, she was already

perceiving results. And yet she was not a satisfactory pupil, in the ordinary meaning of the phrase; she was not the wonder her aunt had hoped she would be; she was not laborious; she could not apply herself to regular study; she detested geography, and was incapable in arithmetic. But her memory was so sure, her perceptivity so rapid, her opportunities so varied and so extended, that she could not help acquiring many sorts of knowledge. Her aunt had tried to direct her, but, of course, had failed, had lost control over her, and thought of nothing but to give her pleasure, to make her brilliant, and to be proud of her. She was not at all "brought up"; no girl could be less so; she blossomed.

Miss Brandon had been persuaded by Madame Hoche, who was a woman with ideas, that "education by contact," in the rare cases where it is materially applicable, is infinitely more easy and infinitely more productive than education by books. Mere "instruction" appeared to her to be a decidedly inferior object to pursue; anybody could learn printed facts; her Claire was to rise higher; she did not know exactly how, but Madame Hoche

said she would, and it was pleasant to believe
her. And all this fitted in, too, with the
vague fancy of "teaching by absorption"
which Harriet Brandon, in her first well-
remembered dream of the training she would
give Claire, had allowed herself to indulge.

In all ordinary cases these notions would
have been fantastic, and even dangerous; they
would have upset the balance of the girls on
whom they were essayed, and have produced
pure damage. But Claire was a special example. By the exciting atmosphere she
breathed, by the almost unlimited facilities
that were at her disposal, by the exceptional
advantages of her position and mode of life,
she was placed in altogether personal conditions of development. At Venice she found
herself in a forcing-house, with every variety
of cultivation going on around her. Her
aunt, after some instinctive resistance, had
taken to Venetian ways and had consented to
make acquaintances. She had got to like the
mixture of types, of manners, of nationalities,
of subjects, of impressions, which she found in
her path. She had become less British and
more European ; her prejudices had diminished,

her sympathies had expanded; she had cast off the skin of Harriet Brandon of Hurley. Time, new habits, the flattering courtesy and attention of which she was the object in consequence of her fortune (which she was beginning to spend largely), had gradually warmed her heart to foreign life. Her drawing-room was one of the centres of Venice, and Claire, since she was thirteen, had her place in the drawing-room.

The fertilising, stimulating action of cosmopolitanism was therefore in full work on Claire. She thought she was in the element she was made for. She had always detested the drudgery of the schoolroom, and, even as a child, had felt keen interest in things and people; she cared nothing for other girls, but liked to talk to men and women, and men and women liked to talk to her. Happily, she had her aunt's honest, loyal, truthful nature, and it saved her from being spoilt. Strong, fearless, generous, self-willed, and self-reliant, yet full of grace and feminineness, hot-tempered but profoundly affectionate and devoted, possessing the solidity of the North and the vivacity of the South, Claire Brandon was a girl apart.

Of book-learning she had comparatively little, though she did not dislike reading; but of life-learning she was piling up a stock that rarely comes in the way of children. For languages she had a singular facility; and though she considered them to be mere tools, and did not count them as knowledge, she never lost an opportunity of laying hands on them. She had always been surrounded by foreign gover-nesses and maids, and at ten years old had spoken German, Italian, French, and English. As time passed on she picked up, in the mixed world around her, scraps of several other tongues. She sang—as children sing—in all of them, and felt intuitively, while she was still in short frocks, that song is the most elevating of all the forms in which emotion can be expressed.

Claire prospered in intelligence, in experience, in skill.

Suddenly, one morning, in the full glow of all this brightness and contentment, a letter reached her aunt from Mr Cumber, informing her that Mr George Brandon had left England for Italy, and was known to have the intention of spending some time at Venice.

The news flung Harriet Brandon back twelve years. She had been floating on the current of a sunny stream, amidst flowers and sparkling ripples. She had lost sight, more and more, of the ugly past; she found the present pleasant; she had ceased to dread the future; the fear that Claire might some day learn the truth no longer pursued her; she had wandered into another world and had grown careless and forgetful. The impressions which once had been so intense and seemingly so ineffaceable, had almost faded from her memory; and when, from time to time, they spoke again within her, it was with an enfeebled echo that barely reached her ears. She tried to forget the existence of her brother. Why should she wish to remember him now that everything for herself and Claire had become so changed? To think of the past was to mutilate the present. The wound was cicatrised; it had only left a scar. Yet, in one instant, it was torn open again, even more torturing, from the circumstances under which the blow was delivered, than it had ever been before. That letter destroyed the existence she had built up. A crash of terrifying thunder rolled through her sunny sky. The old emotionality, which had lain by unemployed, rushed up again. Doubts, torments, terrors, unfelt for years, dashed brutally into her head. The whole frightful story resounded from afar. It seemed to shriek at her. And yet the shock did not crush her. She was herself once more after the first awful shudder. Impulse came leaping to her rescue. She clenched her hands and cried out, " We will leave Venice to-morrow ! " And then she sent for Claire and told her so.

Claire stared at her with stupefaction. She exclaimed — " Leave Venice ! Tatte — why ? Leave Venice ! What has happened ? "

Harriet Brandon took Claire's two hands, and, speaking slowly and with agitation, said, " Darling, we leave Venice because . . . because we must . . . because your uncle is coming, and because . . . we cannot meet him."

Claire looked steadily at her aunt. She had often inquired about her parents. She knew that they had died when she was very young. She knew she had " a wicked uncle." She had, in her early days, compared herself to the children in the Tower, because they, too, had a wicked uncle. She had wondered she

was not told more. But she had had, as yet,
no reason for giving serious thought to the
subject. It did not press. This time it
seemed to her that it did press. She asked,
" But why cannot we meet my uncle ? "

Harriet Brandon had not counted that her
anguish at the news of her brother's arrival
was to be followed instantly by a cruel explanation with Claire. The double pressure was
too much for her. She lost her head under it
and answered, wildly, " Because he is a bad
man . . . because he is our enemy . . . because
. . . because . . . I cannot tell you."

Claire looked very grave. It was evident
her thoughts were working deeply. She was
silent for some seconds, and then said, " Because he is our enemy ? Our enemy ? Why
is he our enemy ? Why should he be my
enemy when I have never seen him ? " And
then, after another silence, she added, in a
voice unlike her own, " Tatte, what are you
hiding from me ? "

" Darling, sweet darling, do not ask me,"
sobbed Harriet Brandon, losing her head more
and more.

" Do not ask you ? Then there *is* some-

thing to conceal.   Have I no right to know?
Or are you afraid to tell me?"

Harriet Brandon wrung her hands in bitter
distress, and gazed about her, as if to seek for
help.   But Claire was in no mood to wait.
She reiterated, in a short, sharp tone, and with
a look of determination that frightened her
aunt still more, "Tatte, tell me.   I *must*
know."

"I cannot tell you," faintly articulated Harriet Brandon, rising with difficulty from her
chair, and, in her blind terror, tottering, almost
unconsciously, to the door.

But Claire sprang before her, put out her
arms and held her, and cried, with flashing eyes
and whitened cheeks, "Tell me.   I *will* know."

"Then sit down—sit down—and I will tell
you—indeed I will," sighed Harriet Brandon,
beaten and trembling.

They came back together to their chairs;
Harriet Brandon took Claire's head upon her
shoulder, held her hands, and said, distorting
the truth somewhat in her crushing emotion,
for the first time in her life, but still struggling
instinctively, to tell no lie, "It was when you
were born, Claire.   Yes, it was when you were

born—at least, soon after. Your father was to have Hurley . . . Of course . . . He was the eldest . . . But the General altered his will when he knew that your father had married a French Catholic . . . And you were disinherited . . . And I quarrelled with George because he got the property from you; and nothing can ever bring us together again. He is our enemy . . . That is it, Claire."

"Is that all?" asked Claire, mistrustfully. "Is that all? It does not seem to me, Tatte, that it is all."

"All?" replied her aunt, beginning, with desperate effort, to win back some control over herself. Is not that enough? Is it not enough that you should have been robbed of what belonged to you? It is not all, if you like, in one sense. There is to be added that I quarrelled with George because of this—but I have said that already—and that I have never seen him since, and that I will never see him again, and that we must go away because of that."

"Oh," said Claire, with a long slow breath. And she looked down and thought, with her lips compressed and a strange expression in her eyes.

After a while she spoke again. She said,
with recovered gentleness, "Dear Tatte, you
will tell me all about it at some other time. I
fancy you are keeping something back. My
wish would be to face my uncle. I have no
fear of him. It breaks my heart to go away—
but we will go. Dear Tatte, I love you with
all my soul." And she threw her arms round
her aunt, covered her with kisses, broke away,
and ran out of the room.

Harriet Brandon sat, for some time, almost
insensible. The storm that had burst so suddenly into the midst of her sunshine had thrown
her down and devastated her. She felt vaguely
that she was much older. The effort she had
made to answer Claire had taken out of her
the little strength that had remained in her
after reading Mr Cumber's letter. Claire was
on the path of the secret ! The work of twelve
years appeared to be lost. What was to happen next ? With returning consciousness came
growing terror. Life seemed to be no more
worth living.

An hour passed in torpid suffering. And
then the door opened quietly, and Claire came
in again. Her eyes were red ; her cheeks

were pale ; but she was calm, and smiled tenderly as she advanced. She sat down upon her aunt's knee, put her arms round her, and whispered, "I come to ask you to forgive me, Tatte. It was wicked and ungrateful of me, and I am ashamed and very sorry. I should not have spoken as I did. You are my sweet Tatte. You are my dear mother . . ."

It was the first time she had called her aunt "Mother!"

At the sound of that name, Harriet Brandon's heart stopped beating. She lifted up her hands, placed them on Claire's shoulders, looked eagerly into her eyes, and murmured, "Mother! Say it again, Claire. Say it again."

And Claire, surprised, not knowing all the word meant at that moment to the afflicted spirit of her aunt, repeated, amidst kisses, "Mother! mother! forgive me."

Harriet Brandon lost her head again—this time with joy.

"Darling! My glorious Claire!" she said. "It was so sweet to hear. And yet you must not say it. It does not belong to me. It belongs to the dead. I try to take her place to you, but I cannot take her name. Still, darling, it was so infinitely sweet that I asked, selfishly, to listen once again. That is all. Now it is over. Keep it in your thoughts, for *her*."

"Then you *do* forgive me, Tatte?" whispered Claire, with a caress. "I am so grieved to have caused you pain."

"Forgive you! My child, my light, my life, my all! Indeed I do forgive you. But I have told you everything. I have, indeed. It is because my brother George got Hurley that we left England, and it is because he is coming here that we must leave Venice. We cannot meet him."

"I am ready," said Claire. "When do you wish to start? Shall we come back again, or not? What shall we do about saying good-bye to people?"

"My dear child, we will go as soon as possible—in a couple of days perhaps. As for coming back again, we will see. Of course we shall leave everything here. And we will say good-bye to no one, excepting intimate friends. We will tell them we are going away for a few weeks, to get a change. It does not matter

where. Shall we try Paris? You ought to see
it. Send a note at once to Madame Hoche,
and beg her to come to us directly."

And then Harriet Brandon sat alone once
more and meditated, and, with "Mother" still
echoing in her ears, began to feel more calm.
By degrees she perceived that, as she had
decided to leave Venice while her brother
stayed there, his presence would not, after all,
affect her. She was deeply vexed and angry
with herself for having, in her terror, betrayed
to Claire the existence of a secret; but, even as
regarded that, she hoped, with her buoyant
nature, that no harm would come and that her
foolish admissions might be explained away.
And then the thought of Paris came to her
once more, and she fancied it would be wise to
go there, because the change would be so complete. So, presently, she called again for
Claire, and said, "Now really, darling, I do
think we might go to Paris. Of course it is
a long way; but, once there, it might amuse
you. And, I daresay, it would help for some
of your lessons. As I said just now, you
ought to see it. What do you think yourself?"

"Decide, dear Tatte," was the reply. "You know best. It will soon be too warm for Rome, otherwise I might have asked you to go that way rather. Let us try Paris, if you like. Once out of my dear Venice, all places will be the same to me." Then Claire went away and pondered.

A week afterwards they were established at the Hôtel du Rhin.

.   .   .   .   .   .

Notwithstanding her professed indifference, Claire arrived in Paris with the curiosity which everybody feels when coming there for the first time. She had no sympathy for the North; the existence she had led, and the habits she had formed, had aroused in her the impression that her nature was fitted only to the South, and that she could be content nowhere else. Still, Paris excited her imagination, and, true as was her love of sunlight and of sunlit life, she was really glad to visit it. She hoped, too, to find in it some distraction from the suspicions and the preoccupations which had been aroused in her by the scene with her aunt at Venice. She felt convinced that something was being hidden from her, though she could not imagine what. Her aunt's explanations seemed natural enough in themselves; but the story had been told in such a fashion, with such agitation, such reticence, such hesitation, that less quick eyes than hers would have perceived in it grounds for mistrust. Still, Claire loved her aunt so tenderly, and respected her so deeply, that it seemed to her a wickedness to doubt or to ask questions. So, as doubt persisted in pursuing her, in spite of her struggle against it, she was pleased to change surroundings for a while, in order to renew her thoughts and to escape from the influence of local impressions.

As for Harriet Brandon, the transfer to Paris did not at first bring her the alleviation of anxiety for which she hoped. She continued, notwithstanding the change, to be preoccupied about the possible consequences between Claire and herself of the foolish words she had allowed to escape from her lips. The disposition to make light of troubles had been developed in her by the life she had been leading; but still, the effects of her sudden violent awakening to the risks of the situation remained in her heart, and she carried about with her a certain

constant apprehension, and a deep irritation
against herself. She felt more than all, perhaps, that she alone was to blame for any consequences that might ensue.

Most fortunately for them both they met,
almost immediately after their arrival in Paris,
an old French gentleman whom they had
known intimately at Venice. He was a Count
de Morvan, a retired diplomatist, who had seen
many things, who had acquired much common-
sense and wide experience, who talked easily
and brightly, and who had a particular sympathy and admiration for Claire. He had been
a good deal with her, had probed a long way
into her, and had formed the opinion that, if
she were well handled, she would become a
remarkable person. He had left her with the
idea that he would come across her path no
more, and whenever he had thought of her
since, had regretted that fate had not permitted him to follow her march in life. So
when, to his astonishment, he stumbled on her
in the Rue de la Paix, his satisfaction was
great, especially when he learnt she was in
Paris for a time. He came at once to see
them, offered to be their guide, and told them

where to go and what to look at. To Claire's
complaint that she had the chilly sensation of
having strayed from noonday into gloom, he
replied by arguing that, on the contrary, she
had reached an atmosphere of a curiously in-
vigorating nature, in which, if she liked, she
could inhale new breaths, and from which she
could extract forces that, so far, had been un-
used by her. He declared that Paris, for those
who know how to treat it, is the most teaching
city in the world, the place where ideas are the
most varied, where information is the most attainable, where examples are the most abundant, where resources are the most plenteous.
He pressed Claire to recognise that the disappearance of the cosmopolitan brightnesses, and
of the diversified society she had left behind
her, would be more than compensated, if she
stopped in Paris, by the multiformity and the
facility of the new opportunities she would
enjoy. These opportunities would be of a different character from her previous experiences,
but they would offer, he believed, a higher
utility to her. Still, knowing, as he well did,
Claire's dislike of study and her shrinking from
application, he limited his enumeration of the

means at her disposal to their most superficial
elements; he said nothing of any object that
needed work, and spoke of concerts, lectures,
galleries, and—above all—of talk, as if they
represented the whole educating power of
Paris.

His earnestness amused Claire, and, after a
few days, began to influence her. She let herself
be encouraged to suppose that possibly, after
all, the cold North might give her some new
conceptions, and, as her curiosity was insa-
tiable, she decided to make the attempt. She
promised M. de Morvan that she would not
ask her aunt to go elsewhere at once, but that
she would see honestly what she could extract
from the air of Paris. She added, however,
that she would never be satisfied to stop there
unless they could make friends; for, both to
her aunt and to herself, with their Venetian
habits, the sentiment of isolation would destroy
all local merits, however great.

M. de Morvan listened with keen interest.
He had always had an artist's longing to help
to build up Claire, and what he had seen in
her since they had met again in Paris had
given him the certainty that her character, her

aptitudes, and her wonderful development for her years, promised to produce a woman of rare value. He had exhausted pleasure, he had worn out ambitions, and his emotions were growing languid; but he had preserved much natural goodness. A gentle intellectual dilettanteism, and a particular need of contact with the more delicate forms of feminine endowment and charm, had replaced in him the active sensations of the past. To such a nature there was something very tempting in the notion of contributing to the formation of a temperament like Claire's. He knew that her personality was intense, that her ardour of vitality and her need of productivity were singularly rare. He knew that her long residence in Venice had fertilised her nature, and had prepared it to profit abundantly by opportunities. And, above all, he knew that she had reached an age and a condition of mind in which she required the most careful guidance, and that the outcome of her tendencies and capacities as a woman would depend mainly, if not indeed entirely, on the quality of that guidance. So far, her intelligence had ridden on ahead, interrogatively and somewhat aggressively, like outpost scouts in war time, peering into the visible, watching for the invisible; seeking behind the hills, the trees, the house-tops, for sight of the unknown; desultory, almost disorderly, in its freedom. But now the time had come to try to regulate this somewhat tumultuous enthusiasm. In the opinion of M. de Morvan a rare character might be made or marred by the influence of the next few years on Claire. And, not the least, he knew that Harriet Brandon had neither the head nor the hand required for so intricate a task. So, having confidence in his own skill and nothing to do, he determined, after passing an evening in reflection, that he would endeavour to help a little himself.

CHAPTER VI.

THE next morning M. de Morvan decided that he needed an ally in the enterprise he proposed to undertake. He felt, with his peculiar appreciation of the uses and the powers of women, that he would proceed more safely and more easily if he had a woman to aid him. So, having a sister, he went to breakfast with her.

The Marquise d'Héristal was, in many ways, a remarkable woman. Her experience was wide, her knowledge of human nature was exceptional, her common - sense was sturdy, her selfishness was limitless. She was three years younger than her brother; she had been a widow for twenty years; her only daughter was married, and lived in Poitou. But, though she was alone, she

found life agreeable, and, in order that it
should continue so, she avoided troubles for
herself, and kept resolutely clear of those of
others.   She had an excellent position in the
world, and for the best of reasons ; she was
gay and amusing, said bitter things, and
gave memorable dinners.

As soon as the servants had left the room
M. de Morvan began.   "I have come to
consult you, Juliette.   I fancy that what I
am going to say will interest you.   I think
I told you, when I came back last time from
Italy, that I had met at Venice a curious
English child, that I had been much struck by
her, and that I was sorry to have lost sight
of her.   Well—that child is in Paris, and I
feel, more than ever, that she is wonderfully
endowed, and that there are within her
capabilities which it would be unscientific to
neglect.   She lives with an aunt who, evidently, is rich, and I infer, from words they
have let drop, that their name is a good one
—one of those territorial names, without a
title, which are special to England.   All that,
however, is mere gilding to the frame.   The
picture itself is what has impressed me.   I

want to have a hand in guiding that child."
And then he ceased to speak.

"Go on, Charles," said his sister, finishing
the last drops of her coffee, "I suppose that
is not all."

"Well—all?—no! I should like you to
help me."

"My poor Charles!" exclaimed Madame
d'Héristal, moving from the breakfast-table
to an arm-chair; "my poor Charles! Quite
mad! quite mad! Your own follies are
your own affairs—I never interfere with
them. Your quixotisms are usually harm-
less, and I trust this one will be so too—
though it seems to me to be distinctly more
insane than anything I have known you do.
But if you choose to burden yourself with
cares that in no way concern you, at all
events do not ask *me* to accept a share in
them. Go to some charitable soul. Go to
Henriette de Roche-Charente, or to Marie
d'Argentan, or, best of all, to that vener-
able enthusiast, the old Duchess on the
other side of the street. Go to somebody
who lives for good works. But, Charles,
for the love of common-sense, do not come

to *me*, who never could abide good works. Whatever it be you want of me, I refuse beforehand."

"Just so, Juliette. Of course. May I smoke? I know your views. You have explained them to me on other occasions. I reverence them, as becomes a respectful brother. But I began by saying that my tale would interest you, and, usually, when you are interested you listen."

"Am I to be interested first, and listen afterwards?" asked the Marquise. "Or am I to begin by listening on the mere supposition that I shall be interested? That would be a good deal for even a brother to ask of a woman of experience like me."

"The other night at the Français," replied M. de Morvan, "you declared you were carried away by the scheme of education that Croizette propounded about her niece— you do have emotions sometimes, you know, Juliette—and you admitted even that it would amuse you to have a niece of your own to fashion. I bring you the niece. Is not that interesting?"

"Wonderful! What a brother I enjoy!

And a niece too! A British niece!—all elbows and teeth, I suppose. My dear Charles, you are really too generous; you spoil me."

"Now, Juliette, do remember Croizette. You applauded furiously when she rushed down to the footlights and exclaimed: 'To make a man is the work of every day; to make a woman is a privilege, so infinitely few women are capable of being made.' If that theory pleased you then, why should it not please you now? It pleases *me*, I assure you, and I am delighted to have found an unexpected opportunity of applying it. I propose to you to do the same. It is not often that one gets the chance of transferring a situation from the theatre to real life. Ordinarily, it is the other way."

"You *do* interest me, Charles. Honestly, you do. You are altogether stupendous! How young you are! I could never have invented a niece, even if I wanted one. And what do you propose to do with the niece?"

"The first thing I propose to do is to bring the young lady and her aunt to you—this afternoon, if you will. The second is, that I

want you to get Laure's box at the opera for
me to-morrow night—if she does not use it
herself. I mean to take them there."

"To anybody else I should answer, unhesitatingly, No," returned the Marquise.
"But one has, unfortunately, duties towards
one's family—and that fact has often made
me think it is a great mistake to have a
family. So, to you, Charles, I am forced, out
of decency, to say Yes. But I say it most
unwillingly. I have a vague sensation that
you are leading me to the bottom of the sea."

"Thank you, Juliette. As you are a keen
judge of good talking and good manners, I
think you will be satisfied this afternoon."

At five o'clock Harriet Brandon and Claire,
accompanied by M. de Morvan, entered the
drawing-room of Madame d'Héristal.

The Marquise, who had a very grand air
when she liked, and was a consummate
woman of the world, advanced slowly to
meet them, bowed, did not hold out her
hand, and said, coldly, "I am happy to make
the acquaintance of friends of my brother."
And then she fixed her eyes on Claire with
a hard stare.

Claire returned the gaze with such steadiness and calm, that, after an effort of several seconds, the Marquise could go on no longer, and was forced, to her vexation, to give way.

She said, with marked acerbity, "Are you accustomed to look at the sun, mademoiselle?"

"Only, madame," was the reply, "on the rare occasions when its brilliancy exercises over me a fascination I cannot resist. I have just had one of those good fortunes, and I have ventured to profit by it."

Like most Frenchwomen of the last generation, the Marquise was an enthusiast about forms of talk and well-shaped sentences, and the words used by Claire, impertinent though they were, turned her suddenly from irritation to admiration.

"My dear child!" she exclaimed, "come and kiss me. That is the most charming speech I have listened to since my husband made court to me. Indeed, the Marquis never said anything half so delicate as that."

Claire crossed the room to Madame d'Héristal, curtsied profoundly, and then stooped over her hand and raised it to her lips.

"The language of Sévigné and the manners of Henriette d'Angleterre!" cried the Marquise with enthusiasm. "Charles, I *am* interested. You have more than kept your promise. Sit there, next to me, my child. At least, if you will permit it, madame," added the Marquise, turning courteously to Miss Brandon, whose presence she had momentarily forgotten. "I have to beg your forgiveness for the *distraction* your niece has caused me. She does you so much honour, that I venture to hope you will pardon me for being absorbed in admiration of her."

"You could say nothing," answered Harriet Brandon, "that could give me more pleasure, or go straighter to my heart. I am delighted that it is the sister of our true friend M. de Morvan who speaks to me in that way of Claire."

"Now, what can I do for you and for Mademoiselle Claire, madame? To tell you the truth," added the Marquise, laughing, "I never do anything for anybody—not even for my brother, though I have every reason to believe, so far as I can judge, that I am very fond of him. But Mademoiselle Claire has led me, suddenly, and in a fashion which is new to me, to wish to be of use to her, and the sensation is so strange that I should like to act upon it before it fades. So let me again ask, what can I do for you?"

Miss Brandon and Claire looked at each other. The form in which this declaration was made did not exactly please either of them. Miss Brandon said, however, as if she were delighted, "A beneficent fairy offers us the satisfaction of all our desires. Claire, what shall we ask from the enchantress!"

Claire answered, "I should like to know some French people."

Madame d'Héristal's face turned rather grave again, as she replied, "How old are you, my child? I fancy you have not attained the age at which girls usually enter the world. I can depart from my own rules, but I might not be able, with all the magic power which your aunt so flatteringly attributes to me, to get others to depart from theirs. I could not force open the *salons* of Paris for a girl of fifteen."

M. de Morvan, who, so far, had looked on silently, intervened at this point of the con-

versation : he observed—"If I rightly interpret the thoughts of Mademoiselle Claire,
she has no desire to go into society, in the
ordinary meaning of the phrase. For that she
will wait until her years entitle her to claim
her place. She has been accustomed for some
time, at Venice, to contact with men and
women, and it would be pleasant to her aunt
and herself to continue that contact here."

"That is what I meant to say," added Claire.

"Contact with men and women!" said the
Marquise. "Hum! That is a wide description
of your needs, my dear. But I will see. Will
you all dine with me on Thursday? I will
arrange some 'contacts' for you." And then
they went away.

M. de Morvan put Miss Brandon into her
carriage and returned up-stairs to his sister.

She greeted him with the exclamation,
"*Grand Dieu*, Charles! that is, as you say,
a curious young person. In all my long experience I have not seen a child in whom
there is, evidently, so much, and into whom
so much more may, probably, be put. She is
not pretty—though she may become so later
on—but she is singularly distinguished in

appearance; and as for her manners and her
talk, they are remarkable. She is as self-
possessed as I am, and that, Charles, is saying
a good deal. But—there is a but—to an old-
fashioned woman like me, there is something
difficult to follow in these new products of
education. How did this child become what
she is? It cannot have been by sitting on a
form, as I did, and having her knuckles rapped
—as I did too. I do not suppose she knows
what a form is. After all, is it desirable that
there should be many of her species? The
world, as I have practised it, would go out of
sight if all the girls were like her. You know,
Charles, with all her qualities, she is, undeniably, a little forward and a little impertinent;
and I cannot get myself to believe that for-
wardness and impertinence—however clever
be their shape of manifestation—are desirable
elements of character at fifteen, or, indeed, at
any later age. I have an antique prejudice in
favour of what the nuns at the Sacré Cœur
used to call 'modesty.' The word is a silly
one; it is a nun's word; it expresses inexactly
and insufficiently the deference and subordination which young people ought to show to

their elders; but, for want of a better word, I
use it. This child seems to me not to have
enough of that deference, and to rely too exclusively on herself. I admire immensely the
resolution with which she looked me in the
face just now, and I admire still more the
presence of mind and the intelligence with
which she answered the rough observation I
made to her about it; but, in principle, no
child of fifteen has the right to stare in that
way at a woman of sixty. I admire it, but I
blame it. It was incredibly well done—but
it ought not to have been done."

"May I answer?" asked M. de Morvan.
"You, my dear Juliette, rebel, most naturally, against what you call 'new products of
education'—such products, by the way, are
singularly rare, though I fancy they will
become more frequent in the future. As
things stand at present, I fully understand
your objections. But even if the defects which
you say this child possesses did really exist in
her—which I deny—I should urge, from my
point of view, that it is worth while to have
them, if the qualities to which they correspond
can be purchased at no other price."

"A defect, a price, a purchase, a quality!" broke in Madame d'Héristal. "Why, you are getting into book-keeping, Charles!"

"You purposely distort my meaning, Juliette. You know, as well as I do, that in using the words price and purchase, I am referring simply to the compensations which are the basis of every character. But I repeat my denial of your accusation. Claire Brandon has not the defects which, hastily and at first sight, you attribute to her. I know her very well, and I affirm that she is neither forward nor impertinent. Her nature is very open to impressions, very eager, very manifesting. Those inborn dispositions have been strengthened by the exceptional conditions under which she has been living. It is precisely because she is all this that she needs good guidance now, in order to bring out, if possible, the most perfect fruit from the seed which has been sown in her."

"Well, I will suspend my judgment," replied the Marquise. "I like her. As you said would be the case, she interests me. But if I do consent — in contradiction to all my theories of conduct — to give myself some trouble about the young lady, I shall go to work to smooth her down, and not to push her up. There is enough up in her already."

"There I entirely agree with you. She requires direction, and she is worthy of it. Otherwise I should not disturb the serenity of your existence by seeking to introduce into it a disturbing element of this sort. What group will you collect on Thursday?"

"Ah—yes; we must think of that. It is not easy. I cannot tell people I want them to produce an impression on a child. That would be too absurd. And yet I must choose half-a-dozen talkers to whom she can listen with pleasure, and who will give her a good first impression of French 'contacts.' I like that word 'contacts,' Charles. It is so superbly pretentious. It has in it none of the modesty I was talking of just now. Who invented it? You? Or the child? I shall adopt it. I shall call my dinners 'contacts,' and invite people to do me the honour of 'contacting' with me at half-past seven. For introducing a new word into use, I shall be quoted, in future dictionaries, amongst the founders of the language. Really, I shall

owe you a great deal, my dear Charles, both
now and hereafter. How can I ever repay you?"

.   .   .   .   .   .

The Thursday arrived.

Claire was taken in to dinner by Hugues
de Cresse, a young soldier, a distant cousin
of Madame d'Héristal, and sat between him
and the famous dramatist Orgelle, member
of the Académie Française. The other guests
were Michel Gras the painter, the Duke and
Duchess de Saintes, and Mademoiselle de
Verdon, a ward of M. de Morvan, who was
invited in order that Claire should not be
the only girl.

As happens not unfrequently when effort is
made to obtain a particular result, the dinner
was not a success. It disappointed Claire.
The soldier told her, confidentially, that his
colonel was a brute, and then described to
her a series of recent balls. The Academician
expressed to her the conviction that the earth
would circulate more perfectly through space
if there were no women on it. The painter
mentioned that in his last picture the grass
grew, the birds sang, and the sea roared, and
that the study of that picture would be, for

an ignorant person like Claire, the highest attainable form of art-contemplation. Mademoiselle de Verdon held her tongue, as became a well-brought-up young lady from a convent. The Duchess de Saintes observed three times that the weather had been damp. The Duke told Harriet Brandon that there was going to be an agricultural show, and that he hoped to get a prize for his Normandy pigs. M. de Morvan was out of spirits, and silent. Madame d'Héristal alone talked brightly.

When they drove away, Miss Brandon said, " Well, Claire, if that is all Paris can produce, we have come a long way for nothing."

The next day, Madame d'Héristal called on Miss Brandon, but did not find her. She was told, however, that Claire was at home. She reflected for an instant, and then said to herself, " Well, perhaps that is the best thing that could have happened. I will see her."

Claire received her with the ease of manner and the flow of talk that were proper to her, regretted the absence of her aunt, and hoped that the Marquise would be able to remain till she came in.

Madame d'Héristal answered, "My dear child, I am not sorry to see you alone for a few minutes. I want to make a speech to you. My brother feels a deep interest in you, and he has communicated part of that interest to me. As he is so real a friend of yours, I trust you will not think I am interfering with what does not concern me, if I say a few words to you about yourself."

"Oh, madame," said Claire, "we shall be most grateful to you for advice, and my aunt will be as delighted as I am to see that you are kind enough to think of me."

"Then, my dear child, I will go on. My brother has asked me to throw facilities in your way here ; but, as I told you the first time I saw you, it seems to me, with my French notions, that it is altogether too soon for you to think of the social side of life. I have an old - fashioned belief in what is called 'education'—in the French sense of the word, I mean ; of 'education' as the process which forms character, in distinction from 'instruction,' which is the process that forms knowledge. Instruction is your own own affair. I leave you to decide whether

you will or will not work at books. I cannot
help you there; nor does that side of the
question attract me much. But as regards
education, I fancy I could be of service to
you; and though it is against my principles
to render service to anybody, I feel myself
tempted to make an exception for you. Spontaneous generation — of the sort you have
grown out of—was not known when I was
young. In my time, girls did not leap on to
the stage of womanhood like a fairy out of
a trap. They went through a slow process
of formation, which ended when they were
eighteen. That was the weak part of it—
it ended; as if education could ever end!
But, with that exception, I regard the process
as the right one; and as you have not passed
through it, I am unable to admit—whatever
be your intelligence — that you have been
prepared for life. Nature and opportunity
have done a great deal for you; but neither
nature nor opportunity can produce a complete result without the aid of guidance and
of labour. I doubt whether you have ever
been guided, and I know that you have
never worked. If you are disposed to re-

cognise the truth of what I say, then I
will ask your aunt's permission to render
you such services as I can, while you remain in Paris. But those services will not
be of the sort which, apparently, you have
expected from me. They will be shaped by
my experience of life, and their object will
be to aid you to extract the utmost from
yourself. What do you say, Miss Claire?"

" I thank you most profoundly, madame,
for every word you have just spoken; and
I am touched to the bottom of my heart
by the proof of interest you have given me.
What do you think I ought to do?"

" Ho ! ho !" exclaimed the Marquise; " as
if I could tell you that in detail straight off !
It is easy enough to describe what you have
not done, but to specify what you ought to
do is a very different matter. I can only
say, in general terms, that you ought not
to go beyond your age, as you do now;
that you ought to behave as if you were
fifteen, and not as if you were twenty; that
you ought to be guided, and not to guide
yourself; that you ought to remember you
have an aunt. What will she say to all this?"

"She will think what I think," answered
Claire. "She will——"

"Now, there I stop you," broke in Madame
d'Héristal. "She will think what you think!
What right have you to say that? That is
spontaneous generation again. Let your aunt
think for herself. It is not your business to
think for her. And perhaps she may tell
me it is not my business to say what I
am saying now. You see, my dear child,
you supply me at once with an example
of what you ought *not* to do. What you
ought to do in this particular case—that,
at all events, I can see—is to let me tell the
story to your aunt, and to leave her to reply,
uninfluenced by your domination over her."

"My domination over my aunt!" cried
Claire. "Do you think I dominate my
aunt? Oh, madame, I should indeed be
sorry to believe that."

"Delicious!" exclaimed the Marquise, clap-
ping her hands. "Do you mean to say you
are unconscious that your aunt is your slave?"

"Never shall that be said to me again,
madame!" was the angry reply. "If, in
ignorance, I have led you, or any one else,

to imagine such a thing as that, it shall henceforth be my constant effort to efface the impression. My feelings towards my aunt are full of tenderness, respect, and gratitude. I am ashamed that you can think I dominate her. It pains me; it humiliates me to hear it."

"Decidedly, my dear child," said the Marquise, taking Claire's hand; "there is even more in you than I thought. What you have just said, and especially your manner of saying it, prove that you are as good as you are clever. I did not expect that. Clever people are rarely good. The task of putting you straight will not be difficult. Your faults do not lie deep. I feel quite encouraged. Think over what I have said to you. I will have a talk with your aunt. Meanwhile, remember that I want to be your friend."

As soon as the Marquise had gone, Claire stood still in the middle of the room and thought. She was indignant with herself for seeming to merit the observations Madame d'Héristal had addressed to her, and she was indignant with Madame d'Héristal for making them. But, with the common-sense which formed the basis of her character, and with the judgment which—premature as it was— she had acquired from experience, she was forced to recognise the general truth of those observations. One of them, only one, was, in her opinion, utterly unfounded—the accusation that she dominated her aunt. It was in reality perfectly merited, but she was unconscious of that. The charge wounded her deeply. Her love for her aunt was so intense that she could not comprehend such an imputation. But the Marquise had put it forward as if she believed it; therefore others might believe it too. Claire stared at herself with anger, and said, " It is I, Claire, who have conveyed to others the impression that I dominate my aunt. That is shameful of me ! " And thereon she burst into tears.

While the tears were wet upon her cheeks, the door opened, and her aunt came in.

Claire rushed to her, flung her arms round her, and cried, " Sweet Tatte, Madame d'Héristal has been here, and has lectured me. And I deserve it. And she is going to speak to you about me. But I cannot wait for that.

I am dissatisfied with myself, and I mean to change—from this moment. I was, indeed, dissatisfied before she spoke to me. I have been becoming conscious for some time past that I wanted something—something I could not define. But I can now. I see it plainly. It is that, at my age, I ought to be a child. I have suddenly realised that. Madame d'Héristal has told me, and she is right. I am going to begin my education now— that is, if you approve, darling Tatte. It is rather late; but by working hard, as I intend to do, I may regain lost time. And above all, dearest, I mean to make you very happy, and to be your loving, obedient child. And I want you—*you*—to help me." And they kissed each other many times, and felt that affection is a great good.

Madame d'Héristal had her conversation with Miss Brandon. M. de Morvan talked to his sister. Both of them offered counsel to Claire. She listened with attention, made few replies, thought much, formed resolutions, asked her aunt if she approved those resolutions, and then begged her to carry them into execution.

The result was that Miss Grant and Fräulein
Vogel, who for some years had been supposed
to be joint-governesses to Claire, obtained
opportunities of returning to their respective
native lands, and that Mademoiselle Serret,
a Belgian, was appointed in their place.

Mademoiselle Serret had passed all possible
examinations, and possessed all possible diplo-
mas. She was even more mad about strict
systems, strict rules, strict hours, and strict
principles, than Madame Hoche had been
about "facilities," "contacts," and "absorp-
tions." She crammed knowledge into her
pupils as a manufacturer of *foie gras* stuffs
food into his poultry. She regarded teaching
as a crocodile regards its teeth—as a means of
crunching out individuality. She was utterly
insupportable and detestable. And those were
the reasons why Claire asked to be placed
under her direction. She told her aunt she
wanted to give herself a period of discipline.

Finally, it was agreed that they should stop
in Paris for a while. They sent to Venice for
their belongings, and established themselves in
an apartment in the Rue St Florentin.

There Claire threw herself, with the ardour

of her nature, into resolute study. Excepting
Madame d'Héristal and M. de Morvan, she
saw no one. She worked at everything at
once ; and above all, she laboured, with unfailing purpose, to lead her own thoughts into
order and subordination. She analysed her
feelings with a feverish desire to attain the
" modesty " which Madame d'Héristal had told
her, in one of their conversations, she did not
possess. And after long communing with herself, she finished by perceiving that the liberty
she had once thought so necessary may grow
into a burden rather than a joy, and that in
the reality of life it is often a privilege to obey
rather than to command.

And she became obedient, not by nature,
but from reflection.

Her petulance, her precocity, her forward-
ness disappeared. Her enthusiasm was less
passionate. Her will remained in all its force,
but it was no longer impetuous, and it served
reason rather than feeling. She acquired
steadiness, self-control, and an even balance
of temper.

The hard combat with herself lasted four
years. She continued it resolutely until she

had won. The struggle was full of varied and constantly recurring difficulties, and if she had not been held up by *amour propre*, and by an inexhaustible sentiment of dignity and of duty, she would many times have abandoned it. Religion aided her almost as much as pride. She believed even that it helped her more. Her prayers for constant strength and unfading will supported her; it was in the Madeleine that she sought courage in her moments of exhaustion.

At last one day she said to Madame d'Héristal, who had looked on with wonder at all this, and had become so earnestly attached to Claire that she was amazed at the affection which had grown up in her selfish heart, " You told me to be ' modest.' The word meant more, far more, than I understood when you used it to me. But, thanks to your advice, I have done my best to merit it; and now that I am approaching womanhood, I see more and more how right you were, and how vast is my debt to you. I think I may say at last that I have taught myself to obey and to be silent."

She spoke the truth. The effects of the

change in her were visible in a hundred ways.
But she herself was conscious of it especially
in one particular direction. The longing to
question her aunt about her parents and her
birth had become almost intolerable. And yet
she supported it. On two occasions Berthe
had made accidental allusions to details of
what had happened in her babyhood, and
she was certain that Berthe knew the secret,
if secret there were. Still neither to Berthe,
who had become a sort of foster-mother to her,
nor to her aunt, would she allow herself to say
one word. Harriet Brandon thought she had
forgotten, and it was an immense relief to her
to indulge that belief. But Claire remembered,
and wondered, though she did not speak.

Her nature, which at Venice had been all on
the outside, grew concentrated in Paris. The
influences that surrounded her had changed
completely, and she had forced herself to
change with them.

In knowledge, too, she had made vast progress. Even Mademoiselle Serret—in whose
eyes professors were all dunces, and *savants*
were only smatterers, who was convinced that
since Albertus Magnus nobody had ever

known anything until Mademoiselle Serret
had condescended to appear on earth—even
she was forced to admit that ·Claire had
acquired an extraordinary quantity of instruction. Paris had largely served her. She
had found, as M. de Morvan had told her when
she first arrived, that the atmosphere of Paris
is peculiarly teaching. She had discovered
by experience that the facilities it offers are
not only most numerous and varied, but also
that they are of a nature altogether proper to
the place. She had perceived that the lumin-
ousness, the clearness, the precision which were
once such representative elements of French
intelligence, had left (though they have almost
entirely disappeared) a mark which is not yet
effaced, and that French methods of trans-
mission of thought, French forms of explanation, French processes of intellectual direction,
were singularly exact, expressive, and com-
municative. She felt that she could have
studied nowhere else as she studied there, and
that the action of Paris was especially fitted
to the treatment of such a case as hers. ·By
these advantages she had profited to the
utmost.

Nature had not given her, however, all the capacities she desired, and she suffered from some of her insufficiencies. She had an ardent longing to sing grandly, as the completest and intensest form of outpoured feeling; but, though she was an accomplished pianist, and had acquired a wide acquaintance with music, she had no voice, and could only hum and warble. She could not draw correctly. She had never been able to acquire control over figures, and was very deficient in all arithmetical aptitudes. But notwithstanding these gaps, she had grown, as M. de Morvan had expected, into a most remarkable young woman. To extended knowledge, she united bright penetration and winning goodness; and to employ them all in their full application, she possessed a perfect memory, a brilliant skill of talk, and a universal sympathy with sufferers.

She was tall and very slight. Her features were not regular, and she was too pale; but her face possessed an animation and an expressiveness which more than compensated for the absence of ordinary beauty. Her physical distinction was extreme. Her hands and feet were singularly delicate and slender. The

strange deepness of her eyes, the rare elegance
of her movements, the natural dignity of her
bearing, struck even the passers in the street.
Above all, she carried her head with a
mixture of lightness, grace, and stateliness,
which was special to herself, and which constituted the essential mark of her person.
Nothing could be more characteristic, more
purely and properly individual, than the movements of her neck, and the fashion in which
she threw it backwards.

Madame d'Héristal used to say, "Claire's
head tells the story of Claire's life. Who ever
saw such a descriptive head? All the phases
of her nature are represented in its motion.
When she casts it back with the declaration
of will that the act so evidently implies,
it seems to me that I read in it her whole
temperament. Never was there such a revelation of character by movement. Her
hands are wonderfully eloquent, their power
of narrative is astonishing, but her neck and
head speak out in clearer language still.
They cry her thoughts to the four winds."

M. de Morvan looked on at the success of
what he considered to be his work, with the

delighted vanity of an amateur musician
listening to an opera of his own composition.
He had arrived by degrees at the belief that
it was he who had invented Claire, and that
without his aid she would never have grown
into what she was. It was a solace to his old
age and to his delicately critical spirit to con-
template her development, and to admire in
her, as he thought, the fruit of his own initia-
tive and his own co-operation. He often said to
Madame d'Héristal, " Really, my dear Juliette,
we have reason to be very satisfied with what
we have effected. Of all the work of my life,
I think this concluding effort is the most interesting and the most satisfying. We have
between us made a wonderful woman."

And the Marquise was pleased enough with
her own share of the operation to be able to
listen to her brother's rejoicings without con-
tradicting him.

Harriet Brandon was the only member of
the group who was not satisfied. Notwithstanding the changes which had come about in
her character, her inherent preferences were
still in favour of the independence which
springs from self-will, and she could not bring

herself to approve the sacrifice of unruliness by Claire. She had still hidden away in her the old love of stubbornness, the old tendency to impulse, the old trust in " going straight." Time and circumstance had diminished the force of these dispositions, and had largely modified their composition and their effects, but they remained uneradicated, and in her heart she regretted her " glorious Claire" of Venice, the insubordinate tempestuous child whose spirit was so like her own that she had sometimes given herself the joy of thinking that she had inherited it from her. She knew that will was still in Claire as strong as ever; but it had become disciplined will, and discipline to Miss Brandon implied submission, and, therefore, loss of individual value.

Sometimes she talked to Claire about it. But Claire's answers did not convince her. On this one point the aunt and the niece could not agree. Claire knew that she had gained, and said so. But as she had gained by the loss of what her aunt liked best in her, as she had gained by curing herself of defects which in her aunt's eyes were qualities, it was not altogether unnatural that her aunt should mourn over the substitution.

M. de Morvan judged Claire as an art critic of finished women, and saw in her the delightful harvest of his own cultivation.

Madame d'Héristal looked at her as a woman of the world, and was pleased to have helped to add to the general stock of capacity, merit, and grace.

Mademoiselle Serret viewed her as an outcome of machinery, and was satisfied, as the engineer, to have evolved such a highly wrought manufactured article from the somewhat fantastic raw material which had been delivered into her hands a few years before.

Harriet Brandon thought that "glorious Claire" had been too perfect to be improved, and sorrowed that others had come in and changed her.

CHAPTER VII.

"IT seems to me," said Harriet Brandon to Claire, one morning after breakfast, "that our reasons for continuing to stay in Paris are beginning to diminish, and that other places might now be more useful and more interesting to you. What is your own impression, Claire?"

"I was going to say precisely the same thing to you, my dear aunt. How delightful it is to think together, as we do, and to be always one together, as we are! But though we agree, it is for you only to decide. I will stop or go, just as you like."

"Then, let us go, provided we can select any satisfactory place to go to. I do so long for a home. We had one at Venice. We have not had one here. Paris has never been more than a workshop to you, and a waiting-room to me. Not the faintest beginning of attachment to it has dawned in me during all the four years we have passed in it."

"A home!" exclaimed Claire. "Yes, I too should like a home. Now that I am, as Mademoiselle Serret is good enough to say, 'a symmetrically completed fabric,' now that both 'systems' and 'contacts' are less essential for me, why should we not return to England and fix ourselves there?"

"England?" cried Harriet Brandon, with surprise, but without dissatisfaction. "England?"

"Yes, England, Tatte. Why not? We are English."

"We are English, of course," was the reply, "but we have no English ways, and scarcely any English sympathies. And then, as I told you before, I cannot meet my brother. That would be impossible. And how could we be sure not to meet him if we lived in England?"

"Why, by keeping out of his way," answered Claire, laughing.

Harriet Brandon felt scarcely any emotion at this sudden suggestion. Time, changes, new habits, and, above all, the effects of

seventeen years of impunity, had slowly
cured her apprehensions. She took it for
granted that English people had forgotten
"the Brandon case," and that there was no
danger of Claire learning the truth. The
terror which seized her after the trial had
disappeared. It had been suddenly renewed
at Venice for a time, but it had faded away
again. Claire's position was no longer a cause
of anxiety to her. The world accepted Claire
as her brother's daughter, and that result had
grown to be enough for Harriet Brandon.
She lived in security, and thought herself so
safe, that she was no longer afraid of anything
—except of meeting George. On that single
point she remained unchanged. She thought
rarely of her brother, but when she did think
of him, it was with undiminished hate and
with the old longing for vengeance. All the
rest had drifted out of sight.

So, after a silence, she added, "Well, as
you say, why not? I am not sure you will
like it. But we can try. Of course we shall
always travel, even if we have a home. My
own fancy would be to go back to Venice, but
I recognise that there are objections to that

plan. Only, before we decide anything, had we not better ask M. de Morvan if he has any ideas to offer us ? He is so fond of you, and so kind, that it would seem ungrateful to tell him, abruptly, that we are going away. And the Marquise too ; I think we are bound to hear what she has to say."

So that night at dinner (they had formed the habit of dining a good deal with each other), there was a discussion, at the end of which Madame d'Héristal said, "Then, we agree. I recapitulate our united views. You go to England, and as soon as you are settled somewhere, Charles and I will come to visit you. I deeply regret your departure, but I can uphold no argument against it. You have no motive for fixing yourselves in Paris. Its society would not content you, in its present shape. It is indispensable to an old woman like me, for I have spent my life in it, and ties and habits bind me to it ; but to neither of you two, as strangers, could it offer sufficient satisfaction. It has lost both the brilliancy and the charm it once possessed. It has become unreal and hard. The manners of our grandmothers have perished. The young women are taking up equivocal talk. And furthermore, there is very little society at all—even such as it is. The life of Paris is no longer in the drawing-rooms. Indeed, under this odious Government, I see life nowhere in the land. The Republic has obliterated the French. All the great special qualities of the race have disappeared under its baneful influence. No; for outsiders, Paris is no longer worth living in. You are right to leave it — now that you have extracted from it such good as it can give you. I mourn, but I approve. Go to England."

"I mourn so much that I cannot approve," observed M. de Morvan. "I have not the stern philosophy of Juliette, who talks like Mademoiselle Serret. My feelings dominate my reason. It is useless to tell me that you ought to go, for your going will leave in my existence a blank that nothing can fill up. At my age it is not possible to create new objects. You are very dear to me, and you are going. Do not expect me to applaud."

The next day Harriet Brandon wrote to Mr Cumber to tell him the decision, and to say they would be in London in a few weeks.

.   .   .   .

They found themselves, at first, rather lost in London. They knew few people there. The material conditions of life were new to them, and did not satisfy them. The climate and the gloom of the streets depressed them. But as they had made up their minds to give England a serious trial, and, if possible, to fix their home there, they determined to do everything in their power to conquer difficulties. With this object they told each other that it was for them to change, for them to throw off their imported fashions, for them to bring themselves into harmony with English customs and English talk. Just as, at Venice, they would not have been surrounded by society if they had persisted in being purely English, so, in England, it was idle to persevere in being foreign. They determined to try to fit themselves to English life, and, with that purpose, to cure themselves, as much as possible, of the habits and of the prejudices they had contracted abroad.

It did not seem to Claire that it would be difficult to do so. Not only did she wish sincerely to succeed, but she had in her a

growing capacity of adaptability, and she felt
certain she could fit herself rapidly to novel
situations and to fresh usages. She did not
know much of the details of English life, but
so far as she had been able to perceive them,
superficially, there seemed to her to be little
in them that would repel her.

Within the limit of her acquaintance with
them, there was but one single practice to
which decidedly she would not attempt to con-
form. Notwithstanding the schooling she had
passed through, her character remained essentially impulsive, and her ways and manners
were demonstrative. She knew that to be
properly and purely English she ought to
hide her impressions; and this she could not
do, and did not wish to do. The general quiet-
ness of attitude of the English, the absence
of manifestations of sentiment amongst them,
made her angry. It was her conviction that
expression is both the indispensable and the
inevitable outcome of feeling, and she could
not bring herself to admit that wilful calm
and studied immobility can ever become
merits. No argument could persuade her that
placidity is a higher faculty than vivacity.

Her view of behaviour was that language,
physiognomy, and action ; voice, look, and
attitude ; lips, eyes, and hands ; the speak-
ings of the tongue, the variations of the
face, and the movements of the body, should
all co-operate together for the common cause,
all aid each other as mutual and associated
exhibitors of thought. She was convinced
that life would not convey to her the vig-
orous sensations she extracted from it, if
she had to pass it in unceasing repression
of all exterior notifications of herself. She
needed a constant harmony between her outer
showings and her inner sensibilities. And
what she required to set forth in herself, she
desired to behold in others. She had been
accustomed to gather the impressions which
others wished to convey to her almost as
much from their faces and their movements
as from their words. To suppress action was,
in her mind, to enfeeble eloquence, and to
reduce the power of indicating thought. She
regarded gesture as feeling translated into
movement. To manifest emotion was to her
not only a necessity, but a pleasure and a
privilege, and never could she have decided to

submit to the conventionality which leads so many of the English to regard apathy as a high form of virtue. She had been often told that the woodenness which Europe smiles at in them is produced, in great part, by the operation of that most absurd and most unnatural precept. She could not consent to follow it.

But the more she resisted on this one point, the more she determined to give herself an English shape in all other directions. The natural fairness of her judgment, and the particular will which animated her to do her best to become thoroughly English, combined to decide her, again and again, to remove, so far as she could, all obstacles in the way of realising that desire. She saw, more and more, that the task was not difficult. She had heard from many observers that England had been becoming gradually less insular and more European in its ways, and, with her quick perceptiveness, her own eyes saw at once that the differences between her countrymen and foreigners — whatever they may have been in other days —are now so little marked that there is no longer any real barrier of either prejudice or usage between England and the Continent.

She was confirmed in this impression by the testimony of two witnesses with whom they were establishing a new friendship.

When M. de Morvan was Secretary of Legation he had become very intimate with one of his foreign colleagues, M. Valona. They had been together in several posts, and afterwards had kept up constant communication with each other. M. Valona—who, unlike M. de Morvan, had continued in the service—had risen to the rank of Minister, and had been appointed, some years before, representative of his country in London. M. de Morvan wrote to him and to Madame Valona, begging them to go to see the Brandons, and asking their sympathies for them, especially for Claire. They came, were attracted, came again, and came often. They were both singularly full, even for cosmopolitans, of that universal knowledge of European personages and things which is only to be acquired by long practice of political life in many countries ; and from that knowledge and that practice, there had grown up in them a width of view, a sureness of appreciation, and a steadiness of philosophy which delighted

Claire, and helped to reconcile her to London.

The Valonas assured her, with many arguments and examples, that the English have gained immensely, as companions, during the present generation, and that the pleasure of living with them has correspondingly increased. They told her that, according to their own experience and that of many of their colleagues, the conditions of life in London offer now quite as many satisfactions—intellectual, social, and material—as can be found associated in any other capital. And as regards the manner of existence in general throughout the land, they pointed out that from the spreading possession of money, and from the consequent continuous multiplication of the various elements of the middle classes, England presents a far larger and far more widely distributed national society than can be found elsewhere, and, as a necessary result, possesses a greater mass of educated and organised thought than exists in other countries. They asserted that this thought comes out especially amongst the women, who, in the eyes of foreigners, are making

greater progress than the men, and some few
of whom are beginning to use their language
with a brilliancy that is quite new as a British
capacity. They mentioned particularly, as a
marked inducement for new-comers, the cordi-
ality and hospitality which are shown in England to fresh acquaintances, when once they
are accepted. They recognised that the English do not possess the ease of ways, the
elegance of movements, the brightness of tone,
which are discoverable (though only exceptionally) in some of the societies of the Continent. They acknowledged that their manners are often either rough or shy, and that
they have little sprightliness. But they insisted that, viewing the present constitution
of English life as a whole, and weighing its
qualities and its defects, as strangers see them,
the English have profited more than any other
race by the international equalisation of social
capacities, which is one of the marks of our
period. And they concluded their statement
of the case by asserting that residence in
England is beginning to acquire a value and
an attraction which it did not offer in the past,
and which are producing a deep impression on

the foreigners who have an opportunity of measuring them.

These opinions encouraged Claire. She reported them to her aunt, and insisted that, coming from such a source, they presented themselves with special weight. She wanted to be convinced, and went frequently to the Valonas to talk and listen.

At their house she made several acquaintances. Amongst them was a Mrs Gordon, an old woman, with a large knowledge of the world, a fair intelligence, and an impressionable heart. Mrs Gordon was much struck by the brilliancy, the distinction, and the elegance of Claire, and wished to see more of her. So one day she asked Harriet Brandon for permission to call upon her. It happened, on that occasion, that she remained alone with the Valonas after the Brandons had left, and talked to them with warmth of Claire and of the qualities she possessed.

Suddenly, as she spoke, a memory flashed into her, vague and dim at first, but growing clearer and more precise each instant. She pressed her hand to her head, made an effort of remembrance, and then exclaimed, " Brandon ?

Brandon? An aunt and a niece? How strange! Can it be them? Why have I not thought of it before? It must be them! They must be the heroines of the Brandon case! It is wonderful to stumble on to them like this! I had forgotten all about it; but it comes back to me now. It was so many years ago. How old is the niece?"

M. and Madame Valona listened with stupefaction. Of course they did not comprehend one word.

"What do you mean?" they asked. "What is 'the Brandon case'? The niece may be nineteen or twenty. But do, pray, tell us what *are* you talking about?'

"How astonishing!" cried Mrs Gordon, taking no notice of their eager questions. "And how very interesting! Why, your delightful young friend must be the very girl who was disinherited at that trial, and who was declared to be illegitimate — though all England was convinced of the contrary. What a sensation it made at the time! I remember it better and better. Everybody took their side. Everybody felt for them, and said it was a shame. And everybody said the aunt behaved most admirably. By degrees, the story was forgotten. But it all comes back to me now. Of course these are the people; there can be no doubt about it. I ought to have seen it at once."

And at last she told the Valonas the details of the case, so far as she could recall them, and they all became more interested than ever in Claire.

"Well, what will you do?" said M. Valona.

"I will go to them to-morrow," answered Mrs Gordon. "I am sure the sincerest sympathy will be felt for them, and that everybody will be delighted to know them. Opinion was altogether in their favour at the time; and, as I said just now, the aunt did behave so well! There is no prejudice about such matters, and the declaration of illegitimacy against the child will have no influence on her position, especially as she is so wonderfully taking and is to inherit her aunt's fortune. Money always helps, you know, to guide opinion."

The next day Mrs Gordon called on the Brandons. She was full of kindness and goodwill; talked of her desire to be of use

to them ; declared that Claire would produce
a sensation; questioned her in much detail
about the life she had led, and on rising to
leave, after a long visit, said to Harriet
Brandon, "It has been a real pleasure to me
to come to you. And let me assure you
that, in addition to the other motives which
make me glad to know you, I am particularly
pleased to be able — though it is so long
afterwards — to express to you my admiration of your noble conduct in that trial.
All the women of England felt for you and
praised you."

Harriet Brandon stared at her, shrank back
a step, turned very pale, trembled violently,
glanced with dread at Claire, and at last
gasped out, "Oh no, no, no! Do not speak
of it. Pray, pray, do not speak of it. I
cannot—I cannot . . ."

And then it was Mrs Gordon's turn to stare.
Naturally, she had no clue to the cause of
Harriet Brandon's emotion, but she saw she
had made a mistake, and said, in a gentle
voice, "Forgive me if, thoughtlessly, I have
awakened memories which pain you. My
wish was to comfort you. Believe that. Do

come to see me soon, very soon, and let me
hope that I may help to make London pleasant
for you."

Then she was gone.

And the aunt and the niece were alone—
face to face — with something between them
that neither of them could measure.

They looked at each other, hesitating, uncertain, fearing the next moment and the
next word, almost as if each doubted the
other. Some seconds passed, and then Claire
went to her aunt, took her in her arms, and
whispered, "Do not tell me. I do not ask
to know."

As Claire pronounced these unexpected
words, a burst of light broke into Harriet
Brandon. She saw, in an instantaneous illu-
mination of her heart, the use and meaning
of the change that Claire had worked out in
herself. The Claire that had been made at
Venice cried, "I *will* know." The Claire that
had been made in Paris murmured, "I do not
ask to know." And Harriet Brandon perceived
suddenly, at last, that there is a power above
mere ordinary will—a higher, nobler power—
a power of which she was now, in sudden trial,

forced to recognise the value—the power of self-control.

She took Claire's hands and said, with infinite love, " Sweet child, my admirable child ! God bless you ! " And then feeling, both of them, that they needed to be apart for a while, they separated in silence, and each went to her room and thought.

As soon as Claire had shut her door, she sat down and repeated to herself the words that Mrs Gordon had spoken. It was evident, from those words, that her aunt had not told her the whole truth at Venice. All she had said there was that General Brandon had altered his will ; that, in consequence, Claire had been disinherited ; that George Brandon had got the estate, and that, because he got it, she had quarrelled with him. It appeared now, from what Mrs Gordon had said, that her aunt had been mixed up in a trial about something, that she had behaved admirably, and that opinion in England had been excited in her favour. What could that mean ? At Venice Harriet Brandon had been unable to support the coming of her brother. In London she could not support allusion to the trial. Her manner on both occasions had shown the strangest emotion. What could the trial have been about? If her aunt had behaved so well at that trial, why should she fear to speak of it, as manifestly she did? There must assuredly be a secret which her aunt was hiding from her. Under all the circumstances, it seemed impossible to doubt that there was a connection between George Brandon, the trial, and the secret. But if there had been a trial connected with the secret, the secret must have come out at the trial, and if so, everybody knew it—except herself.

After turning all this over, painfully, and at first confusedly, in her head, Claire arrived at the certainty that her aunt was concealing something from her, and that that something related to the Hurley property, and to her own rights of inheritance of it.

As she went on analysing the situation, and seeking to reduce its elements into order, two cruel questions thrust themselves before her— " If, for some motive, my aunt is deceiving me, is it my duty to respect her attitude, to remain deceived, and to make no attempt to discover the truth which she thinks fit to

hide from me? And if it is my duty to remain wilfully deceived, have I the power to
discharge that duty, to stay permanently silent,
and to preserve towards my aunt the confidence,
the gratitude, the tenderness which hitherto I
have felt for her?"

Claire rose, walked up and down the room,
and asked herself unceasingly, "Have I the
force to support this in silence? And if I can
support it now, can I go on supporting it as
an accepted condition of my life, without ever
attempting to put an end to it by obtaining
information? It is useless to begin unless
I am sure I can persevere."

She had no inclination to be violent. She
desired, on the contrary, to be guided solely
by reason, duty, and love. But *could* she
do it?

She sat down once more, took her head
in her hands, and meditated deeply.

While Claire was passing through this
anguish, Harriet Brandon was suffering almost
more. She was overcome by a renewed attack
of wild terror. She had always told herself
that Claire must never know that she had
been declared legally to be illegitimate. Her

CLAIRE BRANDON.

need to hide the secret was almost more intense than ever; it seemed to her too horrible to confess. The idea of getting out of the whole difficulty by simply telling Claire the truth, never entered into her head. The original obstinacy and wilfulness of her nature remained intact, and continued to guide her in the matter. In that respect her character had not been modified, either by her passionate affection for Claire, or by the growth in her— from long-continued safety, and from the life she had been leading — of insensibility to danger until it actually burst upon her. As she possessed no faculty of reasoning or of seeing two sides of a case together, she was incapable of considering whether, now that Claire was a woman, and now that her suspicions had been excited, it would not be wiser and kinder to let her know the facts than to leave her in a suspense which, even if she had the courage and the moral energy to endure it, must, at the best, be cruelly trying to her. All Harriet Brandon felt was that Claire must learn nothing. But she perceived that, in England, the secret was not in her own keeping, and that, at any moment, Claire

might learn it from a stranger. This Mrs
Gordon, a chance visitor, had almost told the
story in her presence. And what would Claire
say presently when they met again? If she
asked the meaning of Mrs Gordon's words,
what answer could be made to her? How
could an explanation be avoided? She had
just said, it was true, that she would ask
nothing; but was it possible to conceive that
she would or could carry out that intention?
She had learnt too much to be able to remain
silent. Oh, why had they come to England?

She suffered so intensely, she was so absorbed and so carried away by misery and
fear, that she became benumbed, stupefied, and
almost unconscious, and scarcely knew where
she was, or what was happening, when suddenly she was aware that Claire had entered
the room.

Harriet Brandon trembled, and had not the
courage to raise her eyes.

Claire went to the window, looked out, and
said in a quiet and almost natural voice, " It
is very fine, aunt. The carriage will be here
in a few minutes. Shall we go for a drive?"
And then she came across the room, and

added, "I have thought it over. I have nothing to say, and I believe I can promise positively that I never shall say anything. Will you go out with me?"

She had gained the battle. Battles, however, leave hurts behind them, and Claire was sorely wounded. She had decided; her resolution did not falter, even for an instant; she was absolutely determined to bear the situation in which she found herself; but the strain never left her; she was pursued everywhere by a mixture of feelings which not only pained her, but frightened her as well. She accused herself of suspecting and mistrusting her aunt; it seemed to her a crime to do so; but struggle as she would, she could not stifle the voice within her. She told herself a hundred times a-day that it was for her aunt alone to judge what she would say or not say; but she was afflicted by the thought that the tender confidence which had so long existed between them had ceased to be complete. She resisted inflexibly the temptation to seek out the truth, but she was unable with all her vigour to crush the idea that she had a right to know it. She was certain she could prove, in the distress which had come upon her, that she had acquired definitive mastery over her will; but she recognised, none the less, that the effort she was called upon to make would test her force to its utmost limit.

Harriet Brandon, too, was much affected. She lived in constant fear, either that Claire, notwithstanding her voluntary promise, would ask questions, or that some stranger would reveal the whole tale. She longed to get away from London; but she did not dare to avow her wish to Claire, lest she should arouse still more suspicious.

They suffered, secretly and silently, side by side, from fear of the situation, and of each other.

At last, when some weeks had passed, Madame Valona came to tell them she was leaving for Ryde, and that she wanted them to accompany her.

Both the aunt and the niece, for different reasons, found relief in the prospect of going elsewhere. Harriet Brandon fancied that, out of London, there would be less danger of tale-bearing. Claire hoped that change of scene might bring her change of thought.

CHAPTER VIII.

THE life at Ryde was new to them, occupied them, and, to a certain extent, tranquillised them. They found several friends, sailed about and were amused. The painful impressions they had brought from London became less acute; they had frequent moments of forgetfulness, and they would have been almost content again, if a mishap had not occurred which stopped their pleasure for a while. In getting out of a boat Harriet Brandon slipped on the landing-steps, sprained her ankle, and had to lie down for a fortnight.

It was the first time Claire had occasion to nurse her aunt. In her inexperience the case appeared to her very grave, and, for forty-eight hours, she refused to leave the room. Preoccupations about the secret vanished from her thoughts, and were replaced by

anxiety for her aunt's health. The doctor
assured her, in vain, that a sprain is not mor-
tal, and that she could go for a stroll without
any fear that she would find her aunt dead on
her return. Finally, however, she was persuaded to go each day with Madame Valona
for a short walk, and as she liked to look at
water and ships, she always went to the pier.

During one of these walks she became aware
that she was followed by a man who looked at
her with undisguised interest. She turned
away from him, as much as she could without
appearing to be conscious of his presence ; but
she saw that he was middle-aged, good-looking, gentlemanly, and that he wore yachting
clothes.

The next day he was there again, and he
walked behind her and around her so persist-
ently, and was so evidently struck by her, that
Madame Valona observed it, and said, laughingly, " My dear, you have made a conquest."

Claire had been accustomed to conquests
since her childhood, and regarded them with
indifference. No man had ever made the faintest mark upon her heart. This new admirer
vexed her, and even, indeed, disgusted her a

little, for she had an instinctive dislike to out-door homage provoked by nothing but her personal appearance. She was not displeased to awaken sympathy by talk, but physical admiration had no value in her eyes. She was therefore offended by the attention she had excited, and begged Madame Valona to return home in order to escape from it.

But each time she went out the same thing happened, and Madame Valona teased her about it, as if it were a serious matter. She said to Harriet Brandon, "The man is quite in love, I assure you. If Claire does not object to a husband of fifty, here is an oppor-tunity for her. He looks miserable; I am sure his peace is destroyed; it would be merci-ful to take him. I do not altogether like his expression, but he is certainly a gentleman. Only he is always alone, and seems to know nobody, which is odd."

"It is irritating and insulting," exclaimed Claire. "I wish he would go away. He is beginning to spoil my stay here."

The man did not go away; he continued his operations; so Claire ceased to take her exercise on the pier, and walked elsewhere.

By the time Harriet Brandon was able to be lifted into a bath-chair, the matter had been forgotten, and they all went again together to the pier, as a matter of course.

They had got about half-way down it when Madame Valona cried, with much amusement, " Why, Claire, here he is again ! Miss Brandon, look ! This man coming towards us alone, in blue, is Claire's adorer."

Harriet Brandon had been pulled down by her enforced stay indoors, and was not in her habitual state of energy ; she was weak and nervous, and turned her head with mere languid curiosity. But the instant she caught sight of the person who was approaching, a change came over her, so violent, so abrupt, so startling, that Claire and Madame Valona sprang to her in alarm, wondering what could possibly be the matter. She had seized the sides of the chair with her two hands, with a wild effort had lifted herself half standing, and breathless, with locked lips and straining eyes, was staring, as if horror-struck, at the stranger. Suddenly she turned white and faint ; her mouth opened convulsively ; her arms gave way ; and, with a low moan, she fell back heavily in the chair. Drops of perspiration burst out on her forehead; her eyes closed; she made a feeble, spasmodic motion with her hands, as if to thrust away an odious object; she muttered, half inaudibly, "George!" And then her head sank backwards, her arms dropped down, and she swooned away.

Claire had scarcely heard the name, but she felt, instinctively, from the effect produced upon her aunt, that the stranger must be George Brandon.

If she had had any doubts about his identity, they would have been removed at once; for as, in anxious excitement, she hung over her aunt, untied her bonnet-strings, and pulled off her gloves, in order to chafe her hands, he pushed through the small crowd that began instantly to gather, and exclaimed, with the clearest signs of agitation and stupefaction, "What! . . . You! . . . Can you be . . .? Are you . . .? You! Good God!" And, in bewilderment and dismay, he stood and gazed alternately at Claire and at the unconscious Harriet Brandon.

For some seconds Claire, in the intensity of her absorption, seemed to be ignorant of his presence ; but suddenly she dropped her aunt's hands, faced vehemently round, advanced a step towards him, looked full at him with an expression of such aversion that he shivered under it, made a movement as if to speak, but checked it, and turning hastily to the man who drew the chair, cried, "Home, home!"

On the way back Harriet Brandon opened her eyes, and by the time they reached Madame Valona's house she had recovered consciousness, and tried, feebly, to ask questions.

"Where is he?" were the first words she uttered.

And then she said, "Oh, Claire, I have seen him! I feel so ill."

She was got to bed as quickly as possible, but as the shock was moral, it was decided that the doctor should not be sent for unless, later on, medical aid should evidently become necessary.

Fortunately she calmed down fast, and at the end of an hour said to Claire, "This is what I feared when we decided to come to England. I told you I could not meet him. I cannot risk a repetition of it. It seems to me that it would kill me. I should like to go abroad again at once."

"Yes, dearest Tatte," said Claire. "We will go abroad again. We will talk about it to-morrow, when you are quite well. Certainly we will go. We will do whatever you wish."

After a while Harriet Brandon fell asleep, and then Madame Valona and Claire left her bedside, and went to the garden together.

As soon as they were far enough from the house to be out of hearing, Claire said, " Dear Madame Valona, let me ask a favour of you. Never speak to me about all this. I do not wish to discuss it. I am sure I can count on your kind silence."

As Madame Valona had no reason for supposing that Claire could be ignorant of her own history, these words were taken by her to mean, simply, that she shrank from talking of the painful position in which she had been placed by the trial. Nothing could be more natural, so Madame Valona answered, " Certainly, my dear child, I will never mention the subject to you." And then they talked, as best they could, of indifferent matters.

Later in the day Madame Valona found herself alone with Harriet Brandon. She thought it right to profit by the opportunity to state that she had become acquainted with the whole story through Mrs Gordon, and that, consequently, Harriet Brandon could count upon her full and special sympathies, and might, if that were any comfort, speak openly to her.

Miss Brandon took her hand, thanked her warmly, and said it was a relief to her to learn this, because it enabled them to talk unreservedly together. And then she went on to say, "I must warn you that Claire knows nothing, absolutely nothing, beyond the mere fact that the estate went to my brother, instead of herself, and that that is why I will not see him. It has been—and still is—my unceasing preoccupation to keep her in ignorance of the effects of the trial on her personal position. Never must she know the truth."

"I am, indeed, surprised at what you tell me," replied Madame Valona. "I took it for granted that she knew all. And, just now, when she begged me to say nothing to her, I thought, of course, that she desired to avoid a subject that must be painful to her."

"She asked you to tell her nothing?" exclaimed Harriet Brandon. "Ah, there is my noble Claire again! Of course suspicions have been aroused in her, but she promised me, voluntarily, that she would make no attempt to discover the truth. And she keeps her promise by entreating you to tell her nothing! What a magnificent character she has!"

"But really, really, is this wise?" asked Madame Valona. "Others may be less prudent than I am. An accident may teach her all, and what then? It seems to me that, in concealing from her the reality of her situation, you may be creating grave difficulties for the future."

"She must not—must not—know it!" cried Harriet Brandon. "Never — never! She knows too much already; but she is still ignorant of the horrible declaration of illegitimacy. I would give my life to prevent her ever learning it."

"Well, in so very delicate a matter, it is for you alone to judge. I will say no more. My affection for Claire makes me wish for nothing but her happiness and good, and you may be certain that I will do everything in my power to assist you in promoting them."

Harriet Brandon had a quiet night, was fairly well next morning, was able to get up, and was wheeled in an arm-chair into a little boudoir on the same floor.

After lunch, as they were sitting together chatting almost gaily, a servant came in to say that a gentleman, who did not give his name, had called to see Miss Brandon, and was waiting in the drawing-room.

The announcement fell amongst them like a bursting shell. Though no name was given, a name rose instantly in all their hearts. How could he dare to come? They glanced with terror at each other.

Harriet Brandon cried, hysterically, "No, no! oh no!"

Madame Valona told the servant that Miss Brandon was unwell, and could receive no one.

And then they looked again at each other, in apprehension and dismay, wondering what would happen next. But no one spoke.

A minute later the footman came up again with a letter. It was addressed to Miss Brandon, and contained these words: " As I expect you will decline to see me I write this beforehand, to entreat you to permit me to say a few words to you. I beg you most earnestly not to refuse, for I have to speak to you of your niece."

When Harriet Brandon had read the letter she handed it, in silence, to Madame Valona, who, after she had seen its contents, told the servant to go away, and to come back in five minutes for the answer.

Then Claire read the letter; and she and Madame Valona went to Harriet Brandon's side, and stood there watching her and waiting anxiously.

She shut her eyes; but the movements of her face showed how deeply agitated she was. At last she spoke, tremblingly.

"He says it is about Claire! What can it be? But . . . if it concerns her . . . have I the right to refuse? Ought I not to face him? You know . . . how the idea of meeting him has terrified me . . . for seventeen years. But . . . now . . . if it is about Claire . . . I cannot say no. I must not think any longer of myself. It seems to me that I am bound to see him . . . whatever it may cost me."

"But, my dear friend," put in Madame

Valona, "really you are not in a condition to go through a painful scene. You are still very unwell. It will make you ill. Would you not prefer that I should see him, and hear what he has to say?"

"Thank you, thank you. No. I am sure it is my duty. I feel it more and more. Instinct tells me so. What *can* he have to tell me about Claire? I *must* learn that. Yes, yes, let me see him at once and get it over. At once . . . at once . . . so that I may know. . . . Delay would be too trying to me."

Claire did not attempt to utter a word. She kissed her aunt and left the room.

Madame Valona turned Harriet Brandon's arm-chair into a convenient position, pressed her hand, rang the bell, told the servant to ask the gentleman to come up, and went away.

Harriet Brandon made an effort to concentrate all the resolution and all the courage of her nature, and fixed her eyes on the door.

Her brother entered. Their eyes met.

That single look sufficed to show Harriet Brandon that he was afraid of her. In one second her apprehensions disappeared. She felt she was mistress of the situation.

She pointed silently to a chair in front of her. But he did not sit down. He looked again at her, almost timidly, and said, " I am grateful to you for allowing me to see you. I have little to say, but I have long wished to say it; and when you have heard it, I think you will recognise that I have a sufficient motive for intruding on you.

" The reasons which led me to deny that Charles was married, did not endure. As time passed on, I began, in my solitude, to doubt the justice of my acts. I finished by seeing clearly that I had done wrong—very wrong. But the wrong had been effected under conditions of such a nature that I was powerless to repair it, even in part, without your aid. I became devoured by self-reproach, and I confess to you that I went to Venice in the hope of meeting you in order to try to tell you this. On getting there I learnt that you had just gone suddenly away, and I was convinced that you had left on purpose to avoid me. That discouraged me. I made no further attempt to approach you, and notwithstanding the suffering and remorse in which I live, I should probably have abandoned the idea of trying to tell you the truth, if hazard—a strange and very painful hazard—had not brought us together yesterday. I inquired where you were staying, and I have come.

"I dare not speak to you of my brother's child. In my sadness she appeared to me, suddenly, as a light on my lonely way. I did not know—I could not know—who she was.

"Now that I do know, and now that, at last, I have an opportunity of telling you what I feel and what I suffer, I am, if possible, even more desirous than before to obtain your assistance in order to undo the wrong that I have done to my brother and . . . to his child. Now that I have seen her, now that I have felt—in my ignorance of the relationship between us—what that child is capable of inspiring, it is impossible for me to continue in the position in which I have been placed towards her.

"I have to say that I wish to recognise her as my brother's daughter . . . with all the consequences of recognition." And then he sat down, heavily and wearily, to listen to his sister's answer.

Harriet Brandon said, speaking slowly, but with no hesitation—" So this is what you wished to say to me about her ! This ! For motives of your own, you denied the marriage, and got the child declared to be . . . I cannot say what. For motives of your own you now want, as you say, to undo your work. In neither case have you been influenced by any consideration for the child or for me; you have cared for yourself alone.

" I recognise that your second motives seem somewhat less unworthy than your first ones ; but they are both equally selfish. You wanted money then, and you disgraced us all in order to obtain it. You want a quiet conscience now, and you propose that I should help you to perform an impossibility, in order that you may obtain that too.

" As you have been a barrister, I presume you know enough of law to be aware that the verdict which declared there was no proof of Charles's marriage can only be reversed by producing that proof. We have no more proof now than we had then. So nothing can be changed. Claire must remain

. . . what you have made her. And you, on
your side, must remain with your conscience
and your remorse — if really you feel either.
You have done your work too perfectly for
it to be possible to efface it.

"I refuse any further communication with
you, and I call upon you to stand out of our
road and to leave me to obtain for Claire, so
far as may be in my power, the place which
you have done your utmost to take from
her.

"I told you when last I saw you, all those
years ago, when you refused the supplications
I addressed to you on my knees—do you
remember, George?—I told you the day of
punishment would come. You say it came
long ago. It will be a day without an end,
for no end can now be put to it.

"You have seen Claire. You know now
who it is that you have so foully wronged.

"I cannot forgive you. The rest is between
God and yourself.

"I beg you to leave me. I have no more
to say."

George Brandon rose. He said, with every
appearance of deep distress—"You tell me it is

idle for me to make proposals to you, because
they cannot be carried into effect. It is precisely because that is true that I needed your
assistance in order to do the best I could.
Alone, I could do nothing at all; but if you
had consented to help me, we two together
might have managed a good deal. My life
has been melancholy and weary; I have lived
apart with my repentance; but I have found
encouragement, thus far, in the hope that
some day I might make amends. Henceforth
I can hope nothing. I can only leave Hurley
to her when I die. Still, I remain at your
disposal for anything I can do during my
life. When you want me, I shall be ready.
Meanwhile I shall suffer more than ever—for,
now . . . I know her."

"I shall never want you," replied Harriet
Brandon. "The utmost you are able to do
for Claire is to bring her back the money you
took from her. And that is precisely what
she does not need. What she does need is
her father's name—she bears mine, remember,
not his—and it is beyond your power to re-
store that to her. Before you deprived her
of it, I implored you to take the money, but

to leave her the name. You refused. She
has to bear the consequences. Do you pretend that you ought not to bear them too?
Live with your remorse, and leave your victims in peace. You need not have disturbed
me for such a communication as this."

She pointed to the door.

Gloomily and slowly, he obeyed her signal.
The door closed behind him.

Claire and Madame Valona were listening
together, in deep anxiety, for the departure
of George Brandon. As soon as they had
heard him go, they ran to Harriet Brandon.

They found her pale, grave, exhausted, but
calm and self-possessed.

She tried to smile at Claire, who knelt at
her side and held her hands. Tears gathered
in her eyes; but they were tears of consola-
tion, not of sorrow, for she felt that the situation had suddenly changed, and that a few
minutes had sufficed to sweep away from her
the fear of her brother which had weighed her
down for so many years.

She said,—"I am glad I saw him. I shall
never see him again, but I am no longer
afraid of him. He wanted to bring about a

reconciliation. That cannot be. I was very right—very right—to see him. But, thank God, it is over. I feel very nervous and very tired—and yet, much relieved. How strange it is that the very thing we fear most should turn out, sometimes, to be an advantage to us rather than a pain!"

As soon as Claire could leave her aunt, she set herself to review the situation; but she could extract no new suspicions from her uncle's conduct. Instinct told her that there must be something she did not know; but, so far, facts had not confirmed the instinct. She blamed herself once more for entertaining any suspicions at all, and told herself it was unworthy of her to doubt. Yet argument did not drive out her hesitations, neither did reason bring back her confidence. There *was*, assuredly, a mystery.

Her doubts did not, however, make her unhappy; they did not even preoccupy her gravely. The elasticity of her nature, the variety of her occupations, her rare power of will, combined to enable her to drive away disagreeable thoughts, and she managed to preserve a steady control over suspicions which would have destroyed the peace of any character less disciplined and less valiant than her own.

She had determined to bear the burden which had fallen on her—to bear it uncomplainingly and unflinchingly, — and, taking things together, it seemed to her that what had just occurred rendered the task a little less severe.

On one point only there had come an addition to her troubles. George Brandon was now a reality to her. He had ceased to be a mere name. She had come to know him as a living man, and she remembered him with such intense repugnance that she feared to leave the house lest she should meet him again. It was therefore an immense relief to her, as well as to her aunt, to learn from M. Valona, who had inquired at the club, that George Brandon had left in his yacht for the coast of Ireland.

And then they had a period of peace, and almost of pleasure. Harriet Brandon had recovered. Regatta time had come. The weather was superb. The days were full of the outdoor amusements which are special to Eng-

land, and Claire was amused by the newness
of the life.

. . . . . .

On a wild night, off Cape Clear, a schooner
yacht, with topmasts struck, and three reefs
down in her lower sails, was staggering and
straining in the sea-way. The wind blew
almost a full gale, and the darkness seemed to
add intensity to the storm. Leaning on the
weather-rail was a man—alone—his arm round
a backstay, to steady him. Drenched with
the spray and rain, half blinded by the squally
gusts, but heedless, and indeed unconscious
of it all, the man stood there in absorbing
thought. There was a tempest within him
as fierce as the tempest without, for he was
torn with doubt whether it was worth his
while to live, or whether it would not be better
for him to go overboard into the black waves
and have done with pain.

Inquiries of that sort rarely produce sui-
cide. Hesitation leads almost always to the
maintenance of life. Or, if it does termi-
nate finally in wilful death, it is only after
a long struggle and a steady accumulation
of motives.

The man — George Brandon — did not go overboard. It seemed to him, on that occasion, that anguish was preferable to extinction. He did not put the matter to himself in those terms, but in effect he arrived at that result.

And yet George Brandon was suffering almost insupportably. His case was simple, and perhaps not rare. Born with a purely selfish, concentrated nature and a calculating intelligence, cold, self-contained, indifferent to the sorrow of others, he had, from his very boyhood, regarded money as the supreme good. To get it, he had broken with his sister, had thrown dishonour on his name, and had offended public opinion. At first he felt nothing of all this. He had won; he had become rich; and for a time the realisation of his dream delighted him, and sufficed to blind him to all else. But as the years passed on, he began by degrees to lose faith in his work. Slowly he was led to recognise that he had employed excessive means, and to ask himself whether the result he had achieved was sufficient after all to justify those means. Gradually his misgivings grew more and more grave; they acquired indeed such weight, that at last they domi-

nated his whole existence, and forced him to
perceive that he had effected an ill-judged
bargain, and that money had not brought him
satisfactions which rendered it worth the price
he had thought fit to pay for it. When he
was poor, he made, like many others, the mistake of imagining that money was the one
need. But when he had got money, he discovered—like many others also—that by itself
it was not enough.

As his mind was essentially analytical and
critical—like most calculating minds—it led
him, in his solitude, to pass his time in examination of his acts, his motives, and his position. From that examination there had grown
up two consequences—the first, a ceaseless
anger against himself for the error he saw he
had committed ; the second, a strange produc-
tion of remorse.

He had been utterly, totally callous. No
nature had ever been more insensible than his
either to moral considerations, to abstract duty,
to family ties, or to affections of any kind.
He had cared nothing, absolutely nothing, for
anything but money, and to obtain it, all
means had appeared to him to be good and fit,

provided only they were not punishable by law. Accustomed to live alone, he had attached no value to opinion. He wanted no one, so he had feared no one. The accumulation of these dispositions had made it seem to him quite natural to deny his brother's marriage, and to illegitimise his brother's child.

And yet all this, which had once appeared so simple and so reasonable, had slowly changed its aspect. A voice had arisen within him, a voice of which the sound was new to him, but of which he recognised the nature, for he had been told of it in childhood, and he knew that its name was—Conscience.

In vain he tried to close his ears to it; in vain he argued and discussed with it; in vain his nature made an effort to drown the new-born cries by shouting louder still. The accusing tones rose steadily in power; they echoed through him; they rang around him; they deafened him; they exhausted him; and, finally, they overwhelmed him. Worn and beaten in the strife, he suddenly gave way. The battle was over. Conscience had got him for her prey.

When once remorse had completely seized him, when once he saw that he could not escape, he tried, with the coolness of his temperament, to make the best of it. He told himself that, as he had evidently to live with remorse, it was his interest to make remorse as little disagreeable as possible. And then it occurred to him that he would play a clever trick on Conscience if he proposed to recognise Claire as his brother's daughter. With that idea he went to Venice, expecting that he would find his sister there, and that she would listen with satisfaction to his offers.

When the attempt had failed, he told his conscience he had done his utmost, and that he deserved a respite. But Conscience refused to be cheated in that fashion, and, to punish the subterfuge, proceeded to torture him even more cruelly than before.

And so George Brandon's life passed on, in bitterness and reproach, until one day, upon the pier at Ryde, he saw a girl.

That girl stirred up in him a strange abrupt emotion. At his first sight of her he trembled, for he felt, instinctively and irresistibly, that between him and her there was a bond. He

told himself it was ridiculous to think so; he
called the common-sense of which he was so
proud, to help him; but he could not master
his inexplicable sensations, and was unable to
drive out the intuition that there was a mysterious link between them. And to this un-
accountable sentiment of affinity there was
added an admiration which frightened him,
for it had been one of the rules of his life to
despise women. Her type was completely
new to him; her wonderful distinction dazzled
him; the regal movements of her head en-
thralled him. He did his utmost to free himself from the spell she cast upon him; but,
despite his efforts, it wound itself round him
more and more each day, until at last, in his
excitement, he imagined, suddenly, that fate
had placed her on his road to lighten his load
of care. From that instant he saw in her a
revelation of purity and of dignity, an incar-
nation of lofty qualities which, in the revulsion
of his spirit, he grew to reverence from afar.
For the first time he understood the stately
calm of duty done, a calm that he had never
known. Each day she seemed to him more
noble, more imposing. Each day the sight of

her conveyed to him a clearer estimate of his fall, a more definite perception of the truth which he had lost, and the vague beginning of a glimmering hope that he might regain it.

And then he learnt, with crushing anguish, that this symbolic figure, this type of lofty attributes, this conception of an imaginary saviour, was Claire—his brother's child, to whom he had done that grievous wrong. And he had seen that, when she knew who *he* was, she had cast upon him a look of horror.

Finally, he had thrust himself upon his sister, and she had refused to listen to his proposals.

Those were the reasons why, that night, amidst the storm, feeling that he could never be forgiven, he gazed at the black waters and asked them if they could give him rest.

CHAPTER IX.

AT the end of August the Valonas quitted
Ryde, and the Brandons found themselves
once more without a destination. The question of a home was still unsettled. They had,
however, been long enough in England to be
able to measure its qualities and its defects
as a resting-place, and there was no reason for
delaying a decision, so far as the principle was
concerned. The selection of the particular
spot was another matter; but if once they
made up their minds to stop in England, the
larger half of the difficulty would be solved.
Claire liked England, English ways and English people, not with the blind prejudice of
ignorant habit, but as a consequence of experience and comparison. She had tried
earnestly to become English, and had to a

great extent succeeded. So she desired to settle down in England.

Her aunt, however, would say neither no nor yes. The reiterated questions of Claire and the Valonas failed to extract an answer from her. At the bottom of her heart she wanted to go back to Venice, for the double reason that life there had pleased her and that she feared England almost more than ever because of the risks of tale-bearing. Furthermore, she was growing nervous, was losing her old stubbornness, and under the combined influence of changed conditions of existence and of the infinite affection which had arisen in her, was drifting by reaction into gentleness. She still had impulses, but they were rare, and their effects did not last. She was beginning to mistrust herself, and to rely on Claire. So, as Claire insisted always on leaving decision to her aunt alone, it became more and more difficult to reach any decision at all.

The result was that they chose no home, and that they found themselves, without knowing why, at Lucerne in September and on the Italian lakes in October. They travelled thence down Italy to Sicily, got to Tunis and Algeria, spent the winter there, and reached Paris, once more, in April.

The Marquise d'Héristal and M. de Morvan greeted them with warm affection, but attacked the spirit of vagrancy which seemed to dominate them, and declared that they really ought to choose a home, if it were only to be able to give their friends an address to which they could send letters.

Harriet Brandon defended herself laughingly against the accusation of vagabondage, and argued that, even if it were true, there was a good deal to be said in favour of a nomadic life. She hated the worries of housekeeping. She pretended there is a delightful sense of freedom in dwelling under tents. She quoted the Spanish gipsy proverb (which she had learnt from her courier in Algeria), " The dog that trots about finds a bone." She made the utmost of a bad case, but admitted, of course, that some day they would settle somewhere.

For the moment, however, they were in Paris, and in the middle of the season there. So Madame d'Héristal asked Claire if she

still wanted to see society; and on her answering that she did particularly wish to see
it, the Marquise said, " Well, my dear child,
there are no objections this time; you are old
enough now to show yourself; I will see about it
at once. Only, remember what I have already
told you. Do not expect too much. Paris no
longer deserves its former reputation of brilliancy and grace. Spend a couple of months
here by all means; but do it solely to collect
experience, and not with any notion that you
are going to be enchanted by ' contact ' with
the French. We are a decaying race; start
with that conviction, and you will not be disappointed. The Duchess de Saintes, whom
you met the first time you dined with me,
gives a ball to-morrow. You shall make your
appearance there. I will tell her I shall bring
you."

The next evening M. de Morvan took the
Brandons to the opera, and they did not reach
the ball till nearly midnight. They found the
rooms full, and, to Claire's astonishment, all
the mothers were sitting in a row against the
walls, and all the daughters in another row
in front of their respective mothers. To her

question as to the motive of this rectilineal arrangement, M. de Morvan answered that in France, in proper society, no young lady is permitted to stray out of her mother's sight, unless it be for a special five minutes to get some lemonade. Wandering with a partner would constitute, in French eyes, an abomination ; and furthermore, would be most dangerous to the young gentleman who lent himself to it, for he might find himself dragged into the unspeakable folly—utterly unworthy of a Frenchman—of marriage with a girl who has no money.

Claire strolled through the rooms on the arm of M. de Morvan (at his age there was no impropriety in the act). Her striking distinction produced a marked effect. Everybody asked who she was, and, of course, everybody inquired immediately about her fortune. Within ten minutes of her entrance the rumour spread that she was very rich, and then the vultures rushed upon the prey : all the young gentlemen came up in a column, got themselves presented by the Duchess de Saintes, and asked for dances, with a view to immediate matrimony.

The one who managed to get up first endeavoured to utilise the start he had obtained, by remarking, with unctuous bows and ostentatious smiles, that it was an honour which touched him surpassingly to be the first partner of a young lady destined to produce an ineffaceable impression on all who met her. He ventured even on the extravagant act of compromising his future altogether, by asking Claire to deign to dance with him again the next night at another ball to which Madame d'Héristal was to take her.

The second, third, and fourth repeated the same language, more or less identically. The fifth, in the hope of pulling up lost time, went so far as to speak of his father's *château* in Dauphiné as a most agreeable residence; and then Claire thought she had had enough of it, and asked her aunt to take her home.

When they said good-night to the Duchess, the latter whispered to Harriet Brandon— "All the mothers are coming to you to ask for her. They think she has got a million a-year. Prepare yourself. There will be sixty proposals before the week is out."

The next day at three o'clock, as Harriet

Brandon and Claire were chatting together, the door opened and the Countess de Leys was announced.

A tall, ugly woman came in, scattering enthusiastic smiles. She held out her hand with overladen joy, and exclaimed — "Dear madame, I had the pleasure—the great pleasure —of meeting you in September at Lucerne. We stayed together at the Hôtel National. Our short acquaintance made such a delightful impression on me that when I heard this morning from my sister, the Countess de Treillezet —who met you last night at the ball of the Duchess de Saintes—that you were here, I ventured to indulge the hope that you would permit me to come to see you." And then she smiled impassionedly, as if she had never known true happiness before, turned to Claire and added — "As for you, mademoiselle, all Paris is talking of you. Never was there such a sensation. Your *début* is an event. Allow me to congratulate you on the brilliancy of your victory. Like Hannibal—or was it Peter the Great?—you have come, you have been seen, and we have been conquered."

Harriet Brandon had listened to all this with a mixture of amusement, bewilderment, and irritation. But she answered courteously —"I am very pleased to see you again. Have you been long in Paris?"

"No—only a few weeks. My home is in Anjou. I am here now on a visit to my sister; and it is, in part, because of my sister that I have hastened to come to you to-day. She has indeed intrusted me with a mission to you . . . a mission which I am very anxious to discharge, but which . . . "—here she looked, with another burnished smile, at Claire—". . . which needs that I should beg the favour of a few moments' conversation with yourself alone."

Claire stood up, threw her head back with the movement that was habitual to her when she decided anything, raised her eyebrows, bit her lips to prevent herself from laughing, bowed slightly to Madame de Leys, and left the room.

" What a manner !" exclaimed Madame de Leys. " How perfectly brought up she is ! What honour she does you ! I really cannot admire her sufficiently. Dear Miss Brandon,

it is about your most adorable niece that I
have come to see you. My sister has a son—
an only son. She worships him, and lives for
nothing else but him. He is such an excellent
son. He is captain in a regiment of hussars
at Lyons. He is thirty-four years old. He
is short, but he is distinguished ; and though
not exactly handsome, he is considered to be
pleasing. He has perfect principles, and is
worthy of the most entire confidence. He has,
for a soldier, a good deal of religion. Several
excellent marriages have been proposed to him,
but he has declined them all, because, like a
man of honour, he has determined never to
accept a wife unless he loves her. He possesses at present £320 a-year, besides his pay,
and, at the death of his mother, he will have
£600 a-year more. He has always assured
his mother that he has no debts. His mother
—my sister—has confided to me the welcome
duty of coming to you to inquire, as a necessary preliminary, whether a marriage between
her son the Count de Treillezet, and mademoiselle your niece, would enter into your
views. Of course, I do not at this moment
lay before you an official demand. That

would be premature. The young people must
see first whether it is probable that they would
like each other . . ." (Here a still more radiant
smile passed over the face of Madame de Leys.)
" All I seek at this moment is to submit the
idea to you, and to ask your impressions."

Harriet Brandon had stared while this speech
was being delivered to her, and stared still
more when it was finished.

"But . . ." she said, "but . . . really . . . I
do not quite understand. Excuse me. Is this
an offer of marriage for my niece ?"

" Certainly, dear madame. At least it is
the first step towards it. Feeling, as everybody must feel, after what happened last
night, that a number of propositions will be
addressed to you at once for the hand of
mademoiselle your niece, we were desirous—
my sister and I — to profit by the happy
accident which has bestowed upon me the
charming privilege of knowing you, to present
our candidate before any other could come
under your notice. The conditions we offer
are exceptionally good, and I allow myself to
indulge the dream that you will consider them
favourably."

Harriet Brandon was extremely offended by this prodigious communication, but that did not prevent her from being amused. " But, madame," she exclaimed, " where is this gentleman ? "

" He is at Lyons," was the reply. "Of course he will appear at once if we telegraph for him. Meanwhile I can show you his portrait if you like."

" Then he was not at the ball last night ? "

" No ; certainly not."

" So, without having seen my niece, he proposes to marry her ? "

" Oh no, dear madame ; *he* does not propose it. That would be quite improper. It is his mother who proposes it for him, through my intermediary. His mother was married in that way. A suggestion was received by her parents from the aunt of a young officer— he was at Lille, that one. It was arranged that he should come up ; that they should go one evening to the circus ; and that she should wear a peacock-blue dress and he a white hat, so that each of them might know which was the other. And they looked through opera-glasses and liked each other at a distance, and they met a few days later, and money matters were satisfactorily arranged, and they were married, and were very happy until he was killed at Solferino."

"This way of proceeding is rather new to me," observed Harriet Brandon, trying to look grave. "And I doubt whether my niece will quite like to be married by such a process. She will probably prefer to choose for herself, as English girls usually do. I think we had better let the matter drop."

"But, dear madame, it is useless to let it drop. It really will not be in your power to let it drop, for all the men will want to marry her," insisted Madame de Leys. "We are in France, where marriages are always arranged in that way, and where rich girls receive several offers each week. It is because your niece has a very large fortune . . ."

"My niece has a very large fortune ? . . ." interrupted Harriet Brandon. "My niece has nothing at all, absolutely nothing. Some day she will have what I have, but at present, of her own she has not one franc."

"She has not one franc !" exclaimed Madame de Leys, looking very blank. "She has not one franc! But then . . . are you really quite sure ?"

"Well, I suppose I ought to know. If I tell you she has nothing, you may safely believe me."

"Oh, in that case, I must, of course, withdraw the proposal. I made it in the supposition that your niece was very rich, and that it would be a desirable marriage for my nephew. He cannot possibly marry a girl who has nothing but expectations."

"We entirely agree, madame," said Harriet Brandon, rising. "I regret that you should have wasted your valuable time. There will be no advantage in continuing the conversation."

Madame de Leys went away, less smiling and less joyous. She looked, indeed, prodigiously angry.

Then Claire was told the story by her aunt, and the two laughed together for an hour.

During the next few days several other overtures of an analogous nature reached Harriet Brandon. They came in all sorts of ways, directly and indirectly, through men, through women, and through priests. But as it got gradually known that Claire had nothing, the offers ceased, the young gentlemen danced with her much less, and society, undeceived, thought her decidedly a mistake.

No one knew that the secret intention of Harriet Brandon was to give £2000 a-year to Claire if she married.

In talking over this amusing experience with Madame d'Héristal and M. de Morvan, Harriet Brandon asked them, " Is it possible that such an astounding proposal as I received from Madame de Leys can be a usual form of action here ?   Surely it must be an outrageous impertinence, which was tried with us because we are foreigners.   Is it the truth that marriages are ever really arranged amongst you in that fashion ?"

"Of course they are," answered Madame d'Héristal, laughing at Harriet Brandon's incredulity.   " There are dozens of such cases every week.   What seems to you to be so extravagant that you imagine it to be a wild exception devised for your special bewilderment, is a most ordinary daily proceeding in France.   Naturally, there are other manners, too, of negotiating a marriage ; but

this particular way—Madame de Leys's way
—is rather a common one. Do not suppose
you have had the privilege of encountering a
curiosity. Nothing of the sort. Madame de
Leys was perfectly exact when she told you
that marriages here are arranged in that way."

"Then, tell me," went on Harriet Brandon,
"does a marriage put together in that fashion
ever turn out really well ? It is such a purely
commercial transaction that I cannot bring
myself to comprehend by what unforeseen
means feeling can be introduced into it afterwards. When a man and a woman come
together for life after a preliminary financial
discussion conducted on their behalf by somebody else—a discussion in which their pockets
have counted for everything and their sympathies for nothing—there must be small probability, I should think, that they can manage,
later on, to love each other, or even to respect
each other."

"What an utterly false view !" exclaimed
the Marquise. "My dear, how little you know
of the realities of marriage ! It is easy to see
that you have not tried it yourself. Why,
it is precisely *after* marriage, when ties and

interests and habits have grown up, that it becomes natural and easy to feel solid and durable attachment. Love based on fancy is a miserably unreliable sensation compared with friendship based on community of objects."

"You will tell me next," cried Harriet Brandon, "that bitter enemies may become fond friends—if only they get married."

"That would not be at all impossible," replied the Marquise. "But let me answer your question. What I have to say is, that no preliminary discussion, whatever be its nature, has, or can have, the faintest action on the working out of marriage. Marriage is a condition so special, so exceptional, so apart from, and so unlike all other conditions; it depends so absolutely for its developments on circumstances, emotions, accidents, and caprices; it involves—if it is to be carried to success—the adjustment of so many contradictory tendencies, the employment of so many untried capacities, and the combination of so many happy chances, that no antecedents can affect it. Prudence, precaution, calculation, probability, all count for nothing in it. It is utterly impossible to foresee its outgrowth, however you may begin it, for the reason that . . ."

" If I could have imagined you would have told me all these abominations, I would never have put my question to you," interrupted Harriet Brandon.

" Now, do let me go on. I say that the motives, the influences, the incentives, the impulses which marriage brings into play, are all special to, and can only arise in, the state of matrimony itself, and are therefore, when they produce themselves, absolutely new to the two persons interested. I say that it is only *after* marriage that they can find out whether they are fit for each other. It is only then that they can become acquainted with the intentions of fate. In every case marriage is, by its inherent nature, a leap in the dark. No matter in what direction you approach it, the result is equally uncertain. You may bound into delight, or you may topple into ruin, or you may smoulder into anything between the two. Any result is just as likely as any other, and just as independent of any measures you may adopt beforehand. Nothing can guide you surely. No intimacy, however solid; no study of character, however complete ; no habits, however ancient ; no affection, however real, can do more than supply a delusive probability. The best of friends may make the worst of spouses ; and, as we said just now, enemies might possibly get on very well together under the cementing action of matrimony. Consequently, my dear friend, do not preach your English notions to me ; and permit me to retain my French conviction that, in a proceeding of which the issue is so hopelessly unfathomable, it is wise—as you can ensure nothing else — to stipulate that the victims shall, at all events, be certain of bread."

"Horrible! horrible! horrible!" cried Harriet Brandon, throwing up her hands.

"Juliette is, as usual, dogmatic and rather cynical," observed M. de Morvan. "But I am afraid I must say also that she is right. It cannot be pretended that English or German marriages, which are the fruit of the operation known as love-making, are one atom more successful in the mass than French marriages which result from what you call a commercial transaction, and in which no love-making is attempted till after marriage. It would be contrary both to the teaching of facts and to the logic of life, to assert that one system turns out better than the other. The testimony of Europe proves that the proportions of failure and success are, in every country, about the same."

"I listen to you both with abhorrence," exclaimed Harriet Brandon. "Your theories are odious. It is disgusting that men and women should be coupled together without love. If you suppress love as the guiding incentive to marriage . . ."

"I do not suppress it at all," interrupted Madame d'Héristal. "On the contrary, I am altogether in favour of it, provided it is established on a solid basis. But I repeat that, however desirable it may be after, it guarantees nothing before."

"If you suppress love as the guiding incentive to marriage," continued Harriet Brandon, "you ought, as a natural consequence, to suppress marriage itself as well; for without love for its motive—pre-existing love I mean—it ceases to be a high moral act; it loses its noble aspects, and becomes a mere ordinary association for vulgar purposes."

" That has been said to me before," answered the Marquise. "I have even heard it argued by enthusiasts that marriage without love is like language without meaning, like daylight without sun, like a garden without flowers. To me, all that is nonsense. What do *you* say, silent Claire ?"

"I elect to marry like an English girl, in the hope of giving and receiving love. I suspect there may be truth in your description of the special difficulties of the married state, but I believe most firmly that love beforehand supplies the surest means of conquering those difficulties. And, really, I have not been inspired, by my experiences of the last few days, with much respect for the arrangement which, in France, replaces the very ancient process of love-making."

" Oh, I do not pretend," answered the Marquise, "that our system is pretty to look at. I frankly admit that love-making is infinitely more attractive to the eye, more amusing to the head, and more satisfying to the heart. Only it is absurd, illogical, unpractical, and perfectly useless as a producer of permanent effects."

"I said just now," remarked M. de Morvan, "that the results of marriage are, on an average, the same everywhere, and that the various ways of arranging marriage have, in reality, no effect on those results. I do not suppose you will deny the general truth of that, Miss Brandon, or that you will pretend, seriously, that marriages are, on the whole, more productive of happiness in England and in Germany than in France?"

"I do not pretend it," answered Harriet Brandon. "I acknowledge with regret, that —so far as my limited experience enables me to judge—married people do not seem to be worse off in France than they are in England. And yet, as they enter marriage without love, they deserve to be utterly miserable."

"I assure you they are not more miserable than others are," continued M. de Morvan. "Marriage rarely brings about great contentment anywhere. There is a general equivalence about the world in the quantities of happiness and unhappiness, as well as of vice and virtue. The forms and details vary with latitude, climate, and surroundings, but the aggregate of the products is substantially the

same everywhere. There seems to be a law
of averages in the results of human action,
a law from which we cannot escape, and which
is steadily enforced by nature without reference to the methods we employ."

"From which you appear to conclude,"
observed Claire, "that, as no methods can
affect the result, methods are, in themselves,
valueless."

"No, indeed, I do not go so far as that,
Mademoiselle Claire. I proclaim, on the contrary, that, though methods cannot be relied
on to produce results, and though we cannot,
therefore, regard them as possessing any value
of principle, they may, all the same, be very
useful to individuals, and may, in special
cases, render real service. I do not doubt
that as regards yourself, for instance, the
method of falling in love will be the best that
you can follow."

"Thank you for the permission," replied
Claire, laughing. "I will inform you, later
on, how that method succeeds with me."

"I differ entirely from my brother on that
point, Claire," said the Marquise, rather gravely.
"I do not like to see you try the experiment

of love; for, with a character like yours,
failure would be serious. You are an enthusiast; and, though you have acquired
considerable command over yourself, I warn
you that, when love comes, self-command is
usually of small utility. If ever you do en-
counter your ideal; if ever your imagination
is really kindled; if ever you do let yourself
go, your love will be a headlong torrent. I
do not like to speculate as to what might
happen if it encountered obstacles. I should
be more confident about your future if I knew
that you intend to contract marriage without
passion, as a reasonable and well-prepared
arrangement."

"My Claire will never lend herself to such
an odious desecration!" exclaimed Harriet
Brandon.

And then the subject dropped.

That afternoon Claire went shopping, and
Harriet Brandon drove to the Bois with
Madame d'Héristal. After some idle talk,
the latter said, "My dear friend, I want to
speak to you, as we are alone, on a matter
which deeply interests my brother and myself,
and which we have ventured to hope you

would have thought fit to mention, of your own accord, to such friends as we are. As, however, you have made no allusion to it, I thought it was discreet to wait for a natural opportunity of drawing your attention to it. I was sure an opportunity would come—and it has come. What we were all saying this morning about marriage in general, and about Claire's marriage in particular, seems to me to have brought about that opportunity. You will probably not be surprised to hear that the Valonas wrote us all the details about Claire's birth, about the trial, and about your brother. Let me say, at once, that if the earnestness of our regard for both of you could be increased by any cause whatever, the touching story we have heard would have produced that effect. But, my dear friend, I do not bring up the question now simply to tell you that our affection for you both is very great. There is something else; something about which Madame Valona tells me she had already spoken to you; something about which we feel, both Charles and I, that it is our duty to offer you our opinion. You have decided, thus far, to leave Claire in ignorance of her legal position. She may have suspicions — you told Madame Valona that she does suspect something—but I believe I am correct in saying that she does not know the real truth. Now, permit me to ask you whether it would not be wiser to tell her what the real truth is? I put this to you, not only because it seems to Charles and to myself (as it did to the Valonas) that, in principle, Claire ought not, at her age, to remain any longer unacquainted with the situation in which the law has placed her; not only because we think it is unfair—and even cruel—to leave her exposed to the risk of a sudden accidental revelation; but especially because, in talking this morning of her marriage, it occurred to me that, when she does marry, you will be forced to state the facts, whether you like it or not. You cannot give her to a husband under a false label. I found in that conversation the opportunity I was seeking; and now, for Charles and for myself, I entreat you to let Claire know her history. It will have to come out some day. It is only just to her, with her nature, that there should be no further delay."

Harriet Brandon had listened in silence. She remained silent for some time after Madame d'Héristal had ceased to speak. At last, in a low voice, she said, "I do not pretend you are not right. Sometimes even I tell myself the same thing. But I cannot do it. I have kept the secret for nearly twenty years. The keeping of it has been the object of my life. I cannot . . . cannot tell it to her. It would make her so unhappy. And I cannot let any one else tell it to her. I may be wrong—indeed, I think I am—but I cannot do it. If she marries, we shall see. Meanwhile let her have peace — while it lasts. Never, never, never can I decide to tell her— unless the necessity is forced upon me by irresistible circumstances. I have the intensest terror of what might happen if she knew the truth."

"Dearest friend," replied the Marquise, " will you let me point out to you two things? the first, that you ought to think of Claire as well as of yourself—I am not accustomed to see you selfish : the second, that, from what the Valonas have told us, you were just as afraid of meeting your brother, until you did meet him; and then you found you were consoled, not afflicted, by the meeting. It might be the same in this matter of Claire."

"Oh, it is so different!" exclaimed Harriet Brandon. "Claire would be ill. She could not bear it. It is not for myself. Do not call me selfish. It is for her. And yet I cannot help fearing what she might think of me and of my conduct in it all. If she blamed me, if I lost her love, it would kill me."

"But, I repeat," insisted the Marquise, "Claire counts for something."

"Claire counts for everything," was the eager reply. "You cannot doubt that I think of her alone. When I talk of myself it is for *her*. I am only another form of *her*. No; for her own sake, I cannot tell her. If it has to come, it will come by the will of fate, but never with my consent."

"Then I shall look on at the life of Claire with unceasing anxiety," said the Marquise. "I shall watch her history with perpetual dread. May God grant that when at last she does learn the truth — for learn it she will and must—it may not be under conditions that will destroy her whole existence ! I have a gloomy presentiment about it, and so has Charles, and so have the Valonas. You are wrong, dear friend ; you are very wrong."

CHAPTER X.

CHANGE of scene and constant occupation had
given Claire so much to think about that she
had in part forgotten the doubts which had
oppressed her during the preceding summer.
Her present life amused her, and as she sought
instruction in amusement, it did not seem to
her too empty.

Society in Paris interested her extremely;
but it disappointed her even more than it interested her. She had not entirely believed
the accounts of it that Madame d'Héristal had
given her; she knew that the Marquise exaggerated sometimes, and she had learnt not to
attach implicit trust to the depreciatory re-
marks about persons and things which flowed
so easily from her lips. She had continued,
notwithstanding her assertions, to expect that,
at least, the society of Paris would present

features, aspects, qualities, proper to itself.
She knew that it had lost the special graces,
the special aptitudes, the special brilliancies
which are said to have been displayed by it
in other days, but she could not conceive that
it had failed to retain a character of its own,
apart from that of other societies. It seemed
to her that, with such an ancestry, with such
a history, with such traditions, it could
not possibly have become dispossessed of all
distinctive attributes, and that some, at least,
of its former properties must have come down
to this generation, unaffected by destroying
causes.

Yet, though she searched with the curiosity
of a discoverer and the faith of a believer, she
could detect nothing in any way unlike what
she had already seen elsewhere. She found in
abundance the usual inequalities of capacity,
the usual diversities of manner and appearance, the usual disparities of tone, attitude,
and conduct; but she could perceive no
general high level, and she was forced to recognise unwillingly, as her examination proceeded, that the society of Paris, whatever it
may have once been, now resembles all other

societies, and can no longer claim a place apart.

She spoke of this one day when M. de Morvan was sitting with them. She said, " I expected more — much more — than this. I could not have supposed that the idea which Europe persists in entertaining with reference to this society, should be so little justified by reality. Everybody fancies that Paris still possesses three superiorities, — talk, manner, and women's dress. But here, amidst it all, with my eyes wide open, I am constrained to own that, so far as I have seen, talk, manner, and dress are, on the whole, no better than in other places. There are some few bright talkers; but so there are elsewhere. There are some few admirable types of manner; but so there are elsewhere. Here, as elsewhere, striking models are rare exceptions. As elsewhere, provincialism, awkwardness, and dulness are the rule. And as for dress, I am sure we have not seen five women who wear dresses suited to and subordinated to themselves; they all commit, on the contrary, the senseless fault of making themselves the lay-figures and the serfs of their dresses. They do not employ their dresses to set off their persons, but rejoice that their dresses are admired, irrespective of their persons."

"Juliette has told you we are a decaying race," observed M. de Morvan. "That is one of her favourite axioms. Like a good deal she says, there is truth in it; but it alone does not explain the fact which you have noticed, that French society has become scarcely distinguishable from the other societies of Europe. There are two reasons for it — I speak, remember, as an old wanderer, not as a Frenchman. The first is, that we have undeniably lost a large part of our former endowments; that is the one which Juliette has indicated to you. The second—which Juliette has not mentioned, because, as she never travels, she has had no opportunity of perceiving it—is that the rest of the world has been climbing up while we have been slipping down, has been acquiring capacities while we have been losing them. Between the two the character of the various societies of Europe has grown generally similar and equal. Like water, it has found a common level. There are still, scattered about, certain local excellences or weaknesses; certain specific aptitudes or inaptitudes, certain peculiarities due to race or atmosphere; but none of them are important enough, or marked enough, to bestow on the society which owns them any real unlikeness to other societies. They are local accidents, not fundamental differences. The national characteristics of all societies have disappeared, like national costumes. Improved education and improved communications have suppressed them both. I have admitted to you that, simultaneously with the operation of these universal causes, the French have fallen separately from their former place. But let me insist that the decline of France, real though it be, is insufficient by itself to explain the collective levelling. It is due far more to the rise of others than to our own decay."

"But yet you do admit that you are decaying," put in Harriet Brandon.

"I admit it because it is useless to deny what everybody sees, and, indeed, what everybody proclaims. Even our newspapers are full of declarations of our decadence. Society has faded like everything else, and, in part, from the same causes. We have ceased to be the most agreeable people in Europe."

" But if others have become more agreeable than they were, there is compensation," argued Claire.

" No, not for us. Compensation for Europe, but not for France. We French do not regain by the improvement of our neighbours what we lose by our own degeneracy."

" But the wide world gains," insisted Claire, " and that is more important. With all my sympathies for France, I had rather see everybody else profit than France alone."

" Pray do not talk political economy, Claire," said Harriet Brandon. " Mademoiselle Serret is no longer with us; so you can leave that alone. Besides, you are not grateful to Paris. When you were working here you maintained it was a wonderfully teaching place; unlike any other, you thought then."

" I think so still, dear Tatte. I do not mean to detract from its many special capacities when I say that its society seems similar to other societies. And that is all I do say. The Duke de Saintes professes that the cookery of Paris stands alone in the world. The

Count de Morvan—now present—has always
assured me that nonsense, scandal, and Gov-
ernments are more abundant, more irrational,
and more transient here than in any other settlement of men and women. The Marquise
d'Héristal informs me that the theatres are
unapproachably perfect. Victor Hugo proclaims that Paris is the 'City of Light.'
Mademoiselle Serret was of opinion that it is
'an intensified condensation of information,'
'a marrow of tuition.' Being unable to verify
these various assertions, I humbly believe them
all. I can see, with my own eyes, that the
houses are particularly white, the air particularly clear, the cabs particularly slow, the soldiers particularly short, the crowds particularly well-behaved. Shall I go on, Tatte?
There is plenty more of that kind to be said.
But none of it affects the question of the absence of superiority in the society of the place."

"No, no, Claire, do not go on. Your list is
too long already. And it is not fair to Paris,
to make an inventory of it, after that fashion.
It is a place to be felt—not to be catalogued.
I never liked it myself; I do not like it now.
But as other people are mad about it, and say

there is nothing equal to it, I suppose there must be something in it; though I cannot see what."

"I think I can explain it to you," said M. de Morvan. "Only this time I speak as a Frenchman, not as a wanderer. It is precisely because, as you say, it is to be *felt*, that it is what it is. The charm of Paris results, not from the spectacle it offers, but from the emotion it excites. I confess that, when it is looked at minutely, numbers of its ingredients have no charm at all in themselves; yet, as parts of Paris, they assume a charm. Elsewhere their ugliness would assert itself through any surroundings. Here it disappears in the general effect. If I went into detail you would attack me; if I quoted examples you would contradict me; if I argued you would dispute with me. So I content myself with your own word, and I say that when once you have *felt* Paris—and many foreigners do feel it—you love it. That is my explanation."

" And a very miserable explanation it is, my dear Count," answered Harriet Brandon. "You explain by the result, not by the cause; by the end, not by the beginning."

" My aunt's objection is very strong," put in Claire; " but I have to make one which is stronger still. If Paris, as a city, as a whole, possesses the mysterious charm you talk of, why does not its society—which ought to be its pith, its essence, its highest demonstration —offer more charm than all the rest? I assert that, on the contrary, it offers less."

" My dear Mademoiselle Claire, is it quite just of you to attack the society of Paris after the very limited experience you have had of it? You have only been in 'contact' with it for three weeks."

" Three weeks suffice for a general impression, my dear friend; and that is all I pretend to have. Surely you will not deny me the right to form a general impression, as a result of what I see. And remember that I have talked to people who have lived for years in Paris, and whose testimony rests on long experience. There is old Madame Arnsberg; there is Princess Mohileff, who has been here for a quarter of a century; there is the Marchésa Tagliacozzo. You will not assert that those three do not know the place. Well, they all have told me that they stop in it for two reasons—it amuses them, and they are accustomed to it.   But not one of those three, or anybody else, has pretended, in answer to the many questions I have put, that — except amusement—there is one single satisfaction to be got here that cannot be found elsewhere."

" Why, amusement is precisely what society most prizes.   If Paris can offer it, in a special shape or quantity, it seems to me that, by that single property, it stands above and apart from all other places."

" Yes, certainly, that would be so if the amusement were based on origins or capacities which no other place possesses, or if the amusement, in itself, were of a particularly high, particularly varied, particularly satisfying character.   But that is not the case at all.   Amusement here is not—according to the information given to me, remember, without speaking of my own short experience—more intelligent, more abundant, or more keen than what many other capitals can offer.   M. Valona—whose opinion will have weight with you—has always told me so.   There are no outdoor pleasures here,—in that direction London is far away ahead of Paris ; and I maintain that the indoor pleasures have not the charm which Europe is good enough to attribute to them. That brings me back again to society—society, I mean, as distinguished from the streets ; indoors, as distinguished from out of doors."

"There, I have already said that I agree with you," replied M. de Morvan. "The charm I was talking of just now, the charm which delights the foreigner almost more than the Frenchman, is the charm of the air, the movement, the general gaiety. As regards society alone, I can only repeat what I stated just now, that the local characteristics of all societies are disappearing, and that the society of Paris, like the others, has lost the distinctive marks it once possessed. Paris remains Paris and still pleases, in spite of the Republic. Its society is no longer its former self, and ceases therefore to exercise any special fascination."

"All the more reason for preferring England as a home, Tatte, even with its horrible climate. I hope you will decide to settle there."

This was one of the frequent observations which Claire made to her aunt about choosing a permanent resting-place. But she produced no effect. Harriet Brandon could not be de-

cided, and she was beginning to invoke a
special argument against England. She had
suffered, for some months past, from an irritation in her throat, and she declared that English air would be too damp for her, until she
was cured. One of her objects in coming to
Paris had been to consult a specialist ; she had
seen one several times, and he had recommended a season at Cauterets and a dry atmosphere for the following winter. She shel-
tered herself behind this advice to postpone
their return to England, and, against such a
motive, Claire could invoke no arguments.
She recognised that she must go on waiting.

For the moment, fortunately, she had the
occupation of studying Paris, and she threw
herself into it with the ardour of her nature.
She visited all its sights ; she looked at many
of its sorrows ; she examined, so far as she
could, the organisation of its manifold chari-
ties ; she learnt from the admirable examples
that came before her eyes the lesson of the
good that she herself might do elsewhere, and
her longing to relieve suffering grew all the
greater by this teaching. And, with this close
observation of the present of Paris, she did her

utmost to explore its past ; she read, with delighted interest, the books that have been published both on its annals as a whole, and on many special chapters and special features of its life ; she tried to measure and to realise the immense effects that have been produced by politics—far more than in any other city—on the development of the history of Paris, and on the formation of the character of its inhabitants; she pored over the collections of old maps belonging to the State and the Municipality, and reconstituted, in imagination, the former groupings and the former aspects of the streets.

Her remarkable power of analysis, assisted by her unfailing memory, enabled her to carry on this double scrutiny with success; and when, at the end of July, the moment came to go away, she had acquired as complete a knowledge of Paris, its chronicles, its temper, and its life, as it is possible for a girl to procure.

She left it with the two feelings which had arisen in her on her arrival three months before, and which had become confirmed by experience—she was deeply interested and deeply disappointed. She saw the truth of the explanation which had been supplied to her by

M. de Morvan, and recognised that though the society of Paris no longer occupies the first place in Europe, Paris itself still pleases, teaches, and amuses more and otherwise than any of its rivals.

At the last moment the doctor changed his mind. Instead of sending Harriet Brandon to the Pyrenees, he recommended her, suddenly, to try Ems. This modification of plans contented Claire. She had never been to Germany, and began at once to study guide-books and to sketch out a visit to Prussia and Saxony after the cure at Ems was finished.

Her friend, Princess Mohileff, had gone to Ems, and it was agreeable to be certain of finding her there on arriving, so as not to be without an acquaintance.

In order to avoid travelling at night, which was beginning to tire Harriet Brandon, they went by Cologne and slept there. Next morning they continued the journey.

When they entered the carriage they found themselves with a tall white-haired woman of about sixty, who made immediately an impression on them both. Claire, with her quick perception, formed, almost at a glance, an

opinion of the stranger. She seemed a model
of a distinguished old lady, stately but not
stiff, imposing but not severe, aristocratic but
not haughty. The grandeur and the dignity
of her person were very marked, but the
gracious kindliness of her expression and the
naturalness of her manner removed all hardness. She was simply dressed. Claire was
so much struck by her that she whispered to
her aunt, " Tatte, that is somebody. It is quite
delightful to see such a type. I wonder if she
is going to Ems."

And then she looked again at the stranger,
and looked with such evident interest that the
lady smiled slightly. But she did not speak ;
she took up a book ; and Claire, with some disappointment at finding no opportunity of opening a conversation, turned over the newspapers
she had bought, and then looked out of the
window. The lady went on reading, but
glanced from time to time at Claire.

So they travelled on until the train reached
Coblenz. There they had to change for Ems,
and Miss Brandon's courier, with Berthe and
the maid, came to fetch the bags and cloaks.
On leaving the carriage they saw that the

old lady also was preparing to get out. So Harriet Brandon said to her, in French, "Will you permit my servants to take your things?"

"Thank you very much. My maid is there waiting for them."

And she spoke, in German, to a person who had come to the carriage-door.

Then, to Claire's great satisfaction, the old lady walked with them to the other train, and took a place in the same compartment.

As soon as they had got settled in their new seats, Harriet Brandon said, "I hope it is not for yourself that you are going to Ems?"

"Indeed it is," was the reply. "I have suffered for many years from chronic bronchitis, and I come each summer to Ems to battle with it." After a moment she continued, "I think you are English?"

Miss Brandon smiled and nodded.

"I was a good deal in England in former years. I have many friends there, and am always pleased to find occasion to talk gratefully of your land." And then she looked at Claire, and added, "But you, mademoiselle, if I judge aright, can scarcely be purely English?"

" Yes, indeed. But I have been brought up abroad. I am, however, so heartily English that I am thoroughly content with being what I am."

" That is an excellent condition of mind," replied the lady, " and with which I sympathise, for I live in it myself. I, like you, have always thought—and the experience of a life which has grown long has confirmed my first ideas—that the land to which I belong is the foremost in the world."

" As we have confessed our origin, madame," said Harriet Brandon, " would it be indiscreet to ask you what is that country ? "

" I am Austrian," answered the old lady.

And as she spoke the words a flash of such towering pride passed over her face, that, while it lasted, the habitual sweetness disappeared entirely, and was replaced by a glance that was altogether inflexible.

That look astonished Claire, and even shocked her. Her admiration of the stately calm of the face before her eyes was for a moment destroyed by it. But the charm was too real to be affected by a momentary change of expression, however violent, and she soon forgot that the face had indicated for a passing second a feeling different from gentleness.

The talk went on lightly and gaily until the train stopped at Ems, and then with smiles the Brandons and the lady parted.

On reaching the Hôtel des Quatre Saisons, where they had engaged rooms, they found with pleased surprise that the lady had come there too. They arrived almost together.

In the afternoon the visitors' book was brought to Harriet Brandon that she might inscribe their names, and in it, freshly written, they read, " Countess von Hohenwalden, born Princess von Teplitz-Zeditz."

" Our travelling companion ! " exclaimed Claire. " I was sure she was somebody."

Then they went out to see the place, and to seek for Princess Mohileff.

They found her, after a short search, sitting reading in the gallery. Luckily she was alone. After words of welcome, and inquiries about health and friends, Harriet Brandon asked her, " Now tell us ; who is here ? "

" Who is here ? Well, the Emperor is gone ; but that is an advantage, for the crowd is lessened. Of course there is the usual band of

Germans from the top, the bottom, and the
middle, and from all the countries that make
up the empire. There are traders, soldiers,
functionaries, Jews, and princes. And there are
German women as well as German men; good
women, I daresay—they look it. But their
clothes! You will see. And there are plenty
of my compatriots, and people of all other
races—hardly any of them good-looking. And
there is one Frenchwoman—only one. Since
the war they have abstained. But that one
counts for a thousand, for she never leaves off
talking. You must have seen her in Paris—
the Marquise de Rochedure. She is always
exaggerated, often amusing, sometimes fatigu-
ing. She has an opinion about everything,
and permits nobody else to have one in her
presence. The Germans dislike her, but they
make love to her all the same. It is a need
of her nature to know everybody. She is a
highly developed example of the ideal of the
young Paris woman of to-day. In fact I suspect she is the only one of her sort."

And then, as she glanced down the gallery,
a look of astonishment came suddenly over her
face, and she exclaimed, " Why, here comes

my old friend Madame de Hohenwalden. I did not know she was here."

And the Brandons saw that their travelling companion was approaching

There was a warm greeting, and then Princess Mohileff introduced the Brandons to the new-comer.

Countess Hohenwalden said at once to Claire, with evident amusement, " Decidedly, mademoiselle, it is the will of fate that we should know each other. Three meetings in one day cannot be ascribed to unguided hazard. We travel together ; we lodge together ; and now we find a mutual friend who, formally, tells us each other's names."

" I am much beholden to fate, madame," answered Claire, " for treating me so kindly, and for realising my desire to know you."

" I shared that wish," added Harriet Brandon, " and, like my niece, I thank fortune for satisfying it."

" Then I too ought to be grateful to destiny," said Princess Mohileff, " for having selected me to serve as the last link in the combination."

And they talked till five o'clock, when everybody went to consult the doctor.

In the evening they met again at the con-
cert. Claire was particularly astonished by
the attitude of the people whom she found
listening to a badly executed symphony of
Haydn, as if it were a sermon, with a reverence and a devotion that would not have
been out of place in a church. The indifferent
foreigners who dared to talk and laugh, as if no
sacred rite were being performed, offended
the respectfully motionless Germans. And as
even Claire, with all her love and need of
music, was unable to remain silent, and allowed herself to speak occasionally, she too
excited wrath around her, and perceived that
many of her neighbours were casting looks of
indignation at her. That was her first lesson
in the ways of Germany. As soon as the
piece was over, and she could open her
mouth without danger, she said to Countess
Hohenwalden, " Surely it is absurd to make a
tyranny of music like that, and in a *casino*
too. Music is not a prison rule. It is the
noblest manifestation of free thought. To use
it as a destroyer of freedom is an abomination."

The Countess smiled at the excitement of

Claire, and said, " Have you not heard, made-moiselle, that the object of every Government is supposed to be ' the greatest good of the greatest number' ? A German crowd uncon-sciously applies that principle when it listens to a band. It claims that a foreign minority shall not disturb the peaceful contemplative-ness with which the local majority absorbs harmony."

" Oh, madame," cried Claire, " that is only one more of the many proofs we see about the world of the cruelty of majorities. In all matters of feeling—and music certainly is a matter of feeling—I have an instinctive pref-erence for minorities ; for it seems to me that, as a rule, it is they who represent the progress and the liberty of sensation. Besides, there is something very satisfying to the nerves in being on the rebellious side."

" Then, if you want progress, and liberty, and rebellion all at once, I would suggest to you not to remain in the crowd, but to go outside it when you want to manifest your feelings."

And as she said this, Countess Hohenwal-den looked a little shocked. She added, however, "My son talks that sort of language, mademoiselle. Like you, he proclaims the right of every one to an opinion. I have never been able to admit that. I was brought up in the conviction that we ought to dutifully accept our opinions from constituted authority; and here, as regards the manner of listening to music, the crowd is the constituted authority."

"Where is your son?" asked Princess Mohileff.

"At Vienna at this moment. But he will join me here in a day or two, and will stay with me for a while. He has been much occupied, and needs rest. You know what an enthusiast he is, and how hard he works."

"He is a very noble fellow," said the Princess, "and however much you may differ from him in politics, you have every reason to be proud of him."

"Yes, I am proud of him," answered Countess Hohenwalden. "He bears our name worthily—according to the ideas of the period at least." And the strange look of tremendous

pride passed over the old lady's face once
more. Claire saw it.

Before the conversation could be continued,
there came up to the group an extremely well-
dressed young woman, with a bright, intelligent, but not pretty face, exclaiming, as she
took an empty chair, " Ah, here you are, Princess ! I have been looking for you everywhere."

The Princess named her, " The Marquise de
Rochedure."

She bowed carelessly, and told them, putting
her feet at the same time on the bar of the
Princess's chair, " We dined inside — at the
Kursaal — half-a-dozen of us. It was prodigiously nasty. French cookery executed by
German hands. A sacrilege, my dear Princess." Suddenly, she looked fixedly at Claire,
and said, " But—we have met in Paris ! Yes,
surely. I remember your first appearance at
the Saintes' ball. What an emotion you produced ! We made acquaintance at Madame
de Noyelle's. Do you remember ? We were
neighbours at supper, and I upset my soup.
What are you doing here ? Nothing wrong
with your throat, I hope ? Mine is in a

ridiculous state. Some people say it is because
I talk too much. Are you at the Quatre
Saisons? I am. When did you arrive?
Don't let your doctor burn your throat; it will
do you a great deal of harm. It is amusing
here, in a kind of a way; but the getting up
at seven in the morning is awful; it haunts
me all day, and I cannot sleep at night from
looking forward to it."

Harriet Brandon and Countess Hohenwalden
rose together, and the former said, "The
music is going to begin again. After our experience just now, I think it would be prudent
to move away. Shall we go to the river
terrace?"

As they wandered off, three men came up
to join Madame de Rochedure—two officers
from Coblenz and a young Russian. She
lingered behind with them, and was soon out
of sight.

"Did you see many examples of that sort
while you were in Paris?" asked Countess
Hohenwalden of Harriet Brandon. "I have
heard of what the world calls 'chattering
Frenchwomen'; and I have encountered many

of them. But I do not remember such a type as this one."

"Even in Paris she stands almost alone," was the reply. "I remember now that I have heard of her as a rather exceptional person. Many people find her amusing."

Then they went home, to be ready to get up at seven.

END OF THE FIRST VOLUME.

PRINTED BY WILLIAM BLACKWOOD AND SONS.

www.ingramcontent.com/pod-product-compliance
Lightning Source LLC
Chambersburg PA
CBHW020848020726
47497CB00005B/1310